The Ghost of Grey Fox Inn

Read all the mysteries in the

NANCY DREW DIARIES

∾

Nancy Drew

Drew

DIARIES™

The Ghost of Grey Fox Inn

#13

CAROLYN KEENE

Aladdin
NEW YORK LONDON TORONTO SYDNEY NEW DELHI

ALADDIN

An imprint of Simon & Schuster Children's Publishing Division

1230 Avenue of the Americas, New York, NY 10020

This Aladdin hardcover edition October 2016

Text copyright © 2016 by Simon & Schuster, Inc.

Jacket illustration copyright © 2016 by Erin McGuire

Also available in an Aladdin paperback edition.

For information about special discounts for bulk purchases, please contact Simon & Schuster Special Sales at 1-866-506-1949 or business@simonandschuster.com.

The Simon & Schuster Speakers Bureau can bring authors to your live event. For more information or to book an event contact the Simon & Schuster Speakers Bureau at 1-866-248-3049 or visit our website at www.simonspeakers.com.

Jacket designed by Karin Paprocki

Interior designed by Mike Rosamilia

The text of this book was set in Adobe Caslon Pro.

Manufactured in the United States of America 0916 FFG

2 4 6 8 10 9 7 5 3 1

Library of Congress Control Number 2015955848

ISBN 978-1-4814-6596-0 (hc)

ISBN 978-1-4814-6595-3 (pbk)

ISBN 978-1-4814-6597-7 (eBook)

Contents

Dear Diary,

I THOUGHT I WAS GOING TO HAVE A LAZY end of the summer—boy, was I wrong! Bess, George, and I are flying down to Charleston, South Carolina, to attend the wedding of the year! Bess's cousin Charlotte is marrying a popular news anchor, and their nuptials are the talk of the town. I can't believe we get to be a part of it!

Not only that, we're all staying in a beautiful old house called the Grey Fox Inn. Apparently it has quite a colorful history. Who knows what kinds of things have happened within those walls? I can't wait to find out more!

CHAPTER ONE

~

Here Comes the Bride

"WHAT DO YOU THINK, GIRLS?" I CALLED to my best friends, Bess Marvin and George Fayne. "Should we drive with the top up, or down?"

Bess twisted to look back at George, who was sitting in the backseat of the white convertible we'd just rented from Charleston International Airport. "That's a silly question, Nancy," George said. "It's eighty degrees, the sun is shining, and we're on vacation—put the top down!"

I grinned and pushed a button on the dashboard to lower the car's roof. The South Carolina sun was a welcome change from the stormy late-summer weather back home in River Heights. "It's perfect weather for a wedding!" Bess exclaimed, taking a pair of tortoise-shell sunglasses out of her purse.

"It certainly was nice of Charlotte to give you 'plus two' for the wedding, Bess," I said, pulling onto the main road toward town and enjoying the wind blowing through my hair. "Otherwise, we wouldn't have been able to have this little getaway together." Bess's cousin Charlotte was getting married in two days, and she had invited Bess to be one of her bridesmaids. Because Charlotte was marrying a handsome news anchor, the wedding was all over the news and the Internet—everyone was calling it the wedding of the year. George and I were delighted to come along—maybe we'd even be able to squeeze in a little time on the beach!

"I can't wait for you guys to meet Charlotte," Bess said. "The girl is so organized, I bet she's got the entire wedding planned down to the millisecond. The brides-maid dresses are the perfect warm peach color for this time of year, don't you think?"

I could almost hear George rolling her eyes from the backseat. "What does it matter? It could be lime green or neon orange—boys would still be falling over themselves to talk to you."

"Lime green?!" Bess exclaimed in horror. "Ugh. Well, Charlotte isn't exactly a fashion bug, but at least she picked something more suitable than that."

I shook my head and smiled. Bess and George may be cousins, but they couldn't be more different. I glanced over at Bess, who looked like an old-fashioned movie star, with her dark sunglasses on and her blond hair tucked neatly back into a silk scarf. Bess had been gushing with excitement about this wedding ever since she got the invitation a couple of months ago. Besides all the hype, both families were fairly wealthy, so it was bound to be quite the elegant affair. And more than that, Bess simply loved the romance of it—the flowers, the dresses, the music . . . everything.

George, on the other hand, couldn't have been less interested in the idea of attending a wedding. Charlotte was from the other side of Bess's family, so George wouldn't know anyone there. Even so, she was all too happy to travel to a new city and check out the sights. Wedding or no wedding—it was an excuse for an adventure. Peeking in the rearview mirror, I spied George taking pictures of the passing landmarks with her smartphone, her short black hair flying in the breeze. She was dressed in jeans and a thrift-store T-shirt—the official George Fayne uniform for everyday comfort.

"Check it out!" George called suddenly. "It's Rainbow Row!" I slowed the car as we drove up to a line of beautiful row houses painted in pastel colors.

"Ooh, look at that powder-blue one," Bess cooed. "And there's a pink one too!"

George madly snapped photos until we'd passed the last house, when I stepped back on the gas. "I was hoping we'd get to see that!" she said excitedly. "Did you guys know that Charleston is the oldest city in South Carolina? People often call it the Holy City because of how many churches there are here."

"I guess that makes it a really good place for a wedding," I said, stopping at a red light.

"And because it has such a long history," George added, "it's famous for having a lot of ghosts! Even the place where we're staying is supposedly haunted."

I raised my eyebrow at this and craned my head to look at George. "Did a lot of web surfing on the plane, did you?"

George smirked and held up her hands in surrender. "Guilty as charged, Sherlock," she said. "Another baffling mystery: solved!"

I chuckled as we continued driving through the picturesque streets of historic Charleston. George loves to tease, but the truth is, to me, mystery solving is anything but a joke. Back home in River Heights, I've gotten somewhat of a reputation as an amateur detective—and over the years I've learned that trouble has a way of finding me, no matter where I go.

"There it is!" Bess said, and pointed toward a stately white building up ahead. "The Grey Fox Inn!"

I pulled the convertible into the curving driveway that led to the inn's entrance, and stopped the car to take in our surroundings. The building had two stories, with wide, columned patios wrapping around the entire first floor. The grounds were taken up with lush, sculptured gardens, dotted with stone bird fountains and overlooked by huge, moss-covered trees.

"It's absolutely stunning," I breathed.

"I just hope they have Wi-Fi," George said, jumping out of the car.

As we were pulling our bags from the trunk, a blue sedan came up the driveway and stopped behind us. A petite brunette popped out of the backseat and squinted at us through black-framed glasses. "Bess!" the young woman said. "Oh, I'm so glad you're here!"

Bess smiled widely and ran over to embrace her. "I wouldn't miss it for the world!" Bess took the girl by the hand and pulled her toward us. "I want you to meet my very best friends, Nancy Drew and George Fayne—George is my cousin from the other side of the family back in River Heights. Girls, this is my cousin Charlotte Goodwin—the bride-to-be!"

I reached out my hand to Charlotte, who grasped it firmly, looking me straight in the eye. It was strange—given my two friends, I would have thought Charlotte to be one of George's relations rather than Bess's. Her dark brown hair was cut in a no-nonsense, chin-length bob, and she wore no jewelry aside from the sparkling diamond on her ring finger. Her somber maroon turtleneck and black pants seemed completely at odds with the light and summery city all around us. "Thank you for coming all this way," Charlotte said seriously. "I know it's a long trip from River Heights."

"The pleasure is ours," I replied. "Thank you for inviting us to your big day." I cocked my head as a sweet scent reached my nostrils. "Huh," I said. "What is that smell?"

"Oh," Charlotte's cheeks reddened. "It must be this perfume I'm wearing. It's too strong, isn't it? I hardly ever wear the stuff. I can wash it off if you—"

"No, not at all!" I interrupted. "I was just going to say how nice it was." After her initial delight at seeing Bess faded, I noticed that Charlotte seemed anxious and pale. Was something wrong?

Bess must have noticed too. "You doing okay, Charlotte?" she asked, stepping closer to her cousin.

Charlotte looked startled by the question. "Me? Oh—of course. Why wouldn't I be?" She paused and wrapped her arms around herself, as if she were chilled even as the blazing sun beat down on our heads. "I just . . . I guess you can never really be prepared for something like a wedding," she continued in a low voice. "It's so stressful! Getting all these different people together, hoping they'll get along. And there'll always be something that you didn't plan for—"

"Charlotte!" a voice called from the blue sedan. "Where do you want all these gift bags?"

"I'll be right there!" Charlotte replied. She turned back to us, all business once again. "Some of the other bridesmaids are helping me get everything out of the car," she said. "But you guys go ahead and check in with the front desk; I'll see you inside. Your rooms should all be ready." She started to step away, but then stopped and turned back to us. "Oh! I almost forgot." She reached into the tote she was carrying and pulled out three gift bags. "These contain maps of the area, with restaurants and other attractions clearly marked, as well as some miscellaneous toiletries, in case you forgot anything at home. I included a few historical pamphlets for light reading as well." She handed a bag to each of us, gave a sharp nod, and turned to help her friends unload the car.

"Wow," I said, peeking into the meticulously packed bag as she left. "You were right, Bess. She is organized."

"This is classic Charlotte," Bess replied with a wave of her hand. "She's always been a very serious person, even when she was a little girl. She's pursuing a PhD in history, you know. That's what brought her to Charleston in the first place—and how she ended up meeting her fiancé, Parker. To be honest, I was surprised to hear that she was getting married. She never seemed like the kind of girl who was interested in romance!"

"The right person can turn anyone into a romantic," I said, thinking of Ned, my own boyfriend back home.

We hauled our suitcases up to the front patio of the inn, where several guests reclined in wicker rocking chairs, sipping tall glasses of iced tea. We crossed the threshold into the main foyer, and all stopped to gape. A grand, curving mahogany staircase dominated the room, the steps carpeted in scarlet. The walls were papered in a faded floral print, and the wooden floors shone in the sunlight that poured through the large windows at the rear of the building.

"Not too shabby," George said appreciatively.

"Oh . . . there are Charlotte's parents—Aunt Sharon and Uncle Russell!" Bess said.

A group of people were clustered around a small central table, which had been laid out with glass pitchers of iced tea and tiny sandwiches. The couple I guessed were Mr. and Mrs. Goodwin were both lean and well dressed, and Mrs. Goodwin sniffed at the sandwiches as if she wasn't sure whether to trust them. Bess had told us that Charlotte's family lived in Connecticut—her mother was a real estate agent, and her father worked on Wall Street.

Also standing at the table was a handsome young man with ash-blond hair, dressed in a cream-colored linen shirt and oxford shorts. An older couple stood on either side of him like bookends, a stark contrast to the Goodwins. Unlike Charlotte's parents, these two were short and stocky people; the man had an ostentatious mustache, and the woman wore her bleached-blond hair in a bouffant that looked as if it were hair-sprayed within an inch of its life.

"Well, Parker," the older man was saying, "aren't you going to introduce us to your new in-laws?"

"Sure, Dad," Parker replied, a little awkwardly. He gestured to Mr. and Mrs. Goodwin, saying, "These are Charlotte's parents, Russell and Sharon."

Parker's father stepped forward and pumped Mr. Goodwin's hand with fervor. "Welcome to Charleston, y'all. The name's Cassius Hill—but my friends all call me Cash."

"It's a pleasure to meet you, Mr. Hill," Mrs. Goodwin said, a little stiffly, and extended her hand to him.

But instead of shaking it, Mr. Hill brought her hand up to his lips and kissed it. "The pleasure is all mine, madam," he said playfully.

I watched as Mrs. Goodwin's face paled.

"Allow me to introduce my lovely wife, Bonnie," Mr. Hill said. Mrs. Hill moved to stand next to her husband, her light blue, flouncy dress fluttering around her as she went. "Forget the handshakes," she said in a heavy Southern drawl. "I'm a hugger!" She threw her arms around the startled Goodwins, just as Charlotte came through the door and saw what was happening.

"Oh," she said, clearly dismayed. "I see you all have already met."

"Yes," Mr. Goodwin said, extricating himself from Mrs. Hill's embrace. "We have."

"And they say Yankees and Southerners can't get along!" Mr. Hill chortled, a little too cheerfully. The joke was greeted with a stony silence.

Mrs. Hill cleared her throat and looked around the room, seemingly searching for something to talk about. Her eyes landed on the girls and me. "Now, Charlotte, who are these lovely young ladies?" she asked, stepping toward us.

Relieved to have the focus off her flustered parents, Charlotte pointed us out in turn. "This is Bess Marvin, my cousin—she's going to be one of my bridesmaids. And these are her friends George Fayne and Nancy Drew."

Mrs. Hill nodded politely at Bess and George, but her eyebrows went up a little when she took a closer look at me. "A redhead!" she said, almost to herself. And then a little louder, "How very nice to meet you all." She moved back to the table with her husband and son. Parker began pouring iced tea for everyone, while Mr. Hill regaled the Goodwins with the history of the inn. As he was talking, Mrs. Hill surreptitiously rapped her knuckles three times on the surface of the table. If I hadn't been watching, I would have missed it completely.

Parker saw it too and came over to me with a drink. "Don't mind her," he murmured with a smile. "My mother is extremely superstitious, and this whole wedding thing has her on high alert for bad luck."

"But what does that have to do with Nancy?" George asked.

Parker looked apologetic. "Well, redheads are sort of like black cats. If one crosses your path . . ."

Bess laughed. "Well, Nancy is known to attract mischief wherever she goes!" She went on to tell Parker a little bit about my exploits as an amateur detective.

Parker looked intrigued. "If only you lived in Charleston!" he said. "I would love to interview you for a local color piece."

"Parker is the lead anchorman for one of Charleston's news stations," Charlotte explained. "He was doing a story about the Charleston Historical Society when I was working there as an intern. It's actually how we met." She smiled up at him, and Parker reached over to squeeze her hand.

A moment later Mr. Hill's strident voice boomed out, silencing our conversation. "What's that you were saying, Russ?"

I turned to see Mrs. Goodwin looking stricken. "It was nothing, really—" she started to say.

But Mr. Goodwin interrupted her. "I was saying that this is a lovely inn, but that I still don't understand why we couldn't have the bridal party stay at a less expensive venue."

Mr. Hill's face colored slightly. "Well, sir, I don't know about you, but in my family, we like to give our children the best we can, especially for such a special day."

The room became uncomfortably quiet, and I glanced over at Charlotte. The smile had fallen from her face, replaced once more by that anxious expression she'd worn in the parking lot. It made me wonder if there was more to her nervousness than normal pre-wedding jitters. "I'm suddenly really tired," she announced in a flat voice, turning to Parker. "I'm going up to my room."

"Hey, Char, wait—" Parker called out. But Charlotte shook her head, her lips pressed into a tight line. She set down her glass on a side table nearby, grabbed her suitcase, and climbed the spiral staircase without another word.

Bess and George looked at me, their expressions curious. As casually as I could, I said that we should probably check in to our rooms as well. The Goodwins and the Hills barely acknowledged us as we went off to find the front desk.

"Man," George whispered as soon as we were out of earshot. "Trouble in paradise, huh?"

"It's pretty common for there to be some tension between the bride's and groom's families," I reasoned. "It's probably just nerves getting to them. I'm sure they'll get along much better once all the excitement begins."

"I hope so," Bess said, her eyes filled with concern. "I know Charlotte was worried about the two families getting along, but I didn't realize it was this bad."

Around the corner, we found an older man with salt-and-pepper hair and a close-cropped beard sitting behind a tall desk. "Welcome to the Grey Fox Inn," he said pleasantly. "My name is John William Ross, and I'm the owner here. How may I help you ladies?"

"We're part of the Goodwin-Hill wedding party," Bess replied. "We're just checking in."

"Very good," John William said with a nod. "You'll all be on the second floor. Here are your room keys."

We all picked up our keys—old-fashioned gold ones with fancy handles and long shafts. George leaned in and asked, "So, is it true? Is this place really haunted?"

John William looked taken aback by the question. "Haunted?" he asked.

"Yeah!" George said with enthusiasm. "I read all about it online. This place used to be hopping with ghosts back in the early nineteenth century!"

A strange look passed over John William's face, but then his expression turned to good humor. "It's been a while since anyone has come in asking about ghosts," he said with a chuckle. "This inn hasn't been graced by those kinds of guests in many, many years."

George looked crestfallen. "Okay, thanks anyway," she said with a sigh.

"Were you hoping for a supernatural visitor tonight, George?" I asked as we ascended the staircase with our bags.

"It would have been a nice way to break up all this business of flowers and dresses," she said. "But they've got high-speed Internet, so I guess I'll live."

At the top of the stairs, the landing branched out in two directions, and the walls were inset with beautiful wooden shelves filled to capacity with colorful books. I brushed my fingers against their leather and cloth spines, reading titles like *Behind Parlor Doors: The Story of Old Charleston* and *The City of Three Rivers*. Bess and George went down the long hall to the right, while my room was on the left-hand side. We agreed to meet up again in the main room at seven thirty and discuss dinner plans, after we'd all had a chance to freshen up. On the way down the hall, I passed a room with a bronze plate on the door that read BRIDAL SUITE. *That must be where Charlotte is staying*, I thought.

My room was at the end of the hall, number nineteen. I unlocked the door and stepped inside a beautiful, wood-paneled bedroom. Two stained-glass lamps illuminated a large four-poster bed covered with a cheerful butter-yellow quilt, and a set of vintage cherrywood furniture. I pulled my suitcase onto the bed and began unpacking my things and settling in.

After a long, hot shower and a couple of phone calls—both Ned and my dad always insisted I let them know when I arrive somewhere safely—I cast my gaze out the window and saw that evening had crept up on me. A glance at my phone revealed that it was almost seven thirty, time to meet the girls. I left my comfortable room, locking the door behind me, and was about to drop the key into my purse when a muffled scream pierced the silence of the hallway. I whirled toward the source of the sound. It was coming from the bridal suite!

CHAPTER TWO

An Unwelcome Guest

I SPRINTED DOWN THE HALL AND WRENCHED at the doorknob to the bridal suite, but it was locked. Calling Charlotte's name, I started hammering on the door—but after ten seconds of that, only silence greeted me from inside the room. I hoped that Charlotte had simply seen a mouse and screamed, or something equally innocent—but the longer I stood there, waiting, the more unlikely that became.

I turned to run downstairs to get a key from the front desk and bumped straight into a young couple walking down the hall. "Excuse me," I said automatically.

The woman, who looked to be in her late twenties, was magazine beautiful. She was tall and willowy and had flaxen hair that cascaded halfway down her back. She wore a simple mint-green summer dress accented with a thin silver belt. There was something familiar about her face, but in the heat of the moment, I couldn't pinpoint exactly what it was.

"Is everything all right?" the young woman asked, her eyebrows furrowed in concern. "We heard someone shouting up here."

"I'm not sure," I said quickly. "I heard a scream coming from the bridal suite, and I've been trying to reach my friend inside, but there's no answer."

The woman's face paled. "Charlotte . . . ," she murmured, staring toward the locked room. She turned to the man at her side. "Morgan, that's my sister in there!" she exclaimed.

"Say no more," he said, and marched up to the door.

He wasn't an overly large man, but I could see quite a bit of muscle pushing through his pastel-blue button-down shirt. Morgan, like his companion, was remarkably good-looking. He wore his light brown hair slicked back and had the chiseled, intense face of a soap opera heartthrob.

He rattled the door, testing its strength, before ramming his shoulder into it with great force. The door burst open, sending Morgan barreling inside, with the woman and me following close behind him. The woman let out a little yelp of fear, and I soon saw why: Charlotte was lying in the middle of the room in her bathrobe, unconscious.

Within seconds we were at her side, and after checking her heartbeat and pulse, I was relieved to see that Charlotte was breathing normally and appeared unhurt. "Can you hear me?" the woman said, shaking Charlotte gently by the shoulders. "Wake up!"

After several tense moments, Charlotte's eyes fluttered. "Piper?" she murmured.

We breathed a collective sigh of relief and helped

Charlotte into a sitting position. I filled a cup with water from the bathroom and pushed it into her trembling hands. When the color had begun to return to her face, I said, "I heard you scream from the hallway—what happened?"

"It was the strangest thing," Charlotte said, shaking her head. "I came out of the shower and walked in here to get my glasses from the top of the vanity. But when I looked up at the mirror, I saw a dark figure standing behind me! It was kind of dim in the room, so I couldn't make out much detail, but it looked like he was wearing some kind of uniform. Something old-fashioned. That's when I screamed. I tried to run for the door, but I tripped over my suitcase and must have hit my head against the bedpost on the way down." She rubbed her temple and winced. "That's all I remember."

I sat back on my heels, thinking. It was an outrageous story—particularly coming from someone as sensible as Charlotte seemed to be. Something occurred to me, and I glanced over at the mirrored vanity to confirm it. "Charlotte," I said. "You never got the chance to put on your glasses, did you?"

Charlotte touched her face, puzzled to find it bare. "No," she said. "I guess I didn't. I saw the intruder before I was able to pick them up." She looked back at me, a defensive note creeping into her voice. "I see what you're getting at, Nancy—but I know what I saw. My eyes aren't that bad."

I wanted to believe her, but Charlotte's story just seemed so implausible. Could it be that the stress of the wedding was affecting her even more than anyone suspected? It was possible, but I knew better than to suggest that to a jittery bride-to-be.

A moment later I heard Bess's familiar voice at the door. "Hello?" she said, poking her head in. "What's going on in here? Charlotte, are you all right?" She hurried into the room, with George following behind her.

After assuring Bess that she was fine, Charlotte recounted her story once more for Bess and George. When she heard that Charlotte had hit her head, Bess immediately took off out the door, returning only minutes later with a middle-aged man wearing tiny, round glasses that framed his kind eyes. "Uncle Harry is a doctor," Bess explained. "I thought he should take a look at Charlotte just to make sure she doesn't have a concussion."

"Good thinking," I said to Bess.

While Uncle Harry examined Charlotte, my friends and I retreated to the windows to talk.

"It's a strange story, don't you think?" I asked.

"Strange?" George said, an excited gleam in her eye. "I think it's a great story. You know what this means, right?"

Bess and I exchanged a look. "No," I said. "What?"

"This place might be haunted after all!"

Bess rolled her eyes. "Don't be ridiculous, George. Charlotte didn't see a ghost."

George crossed her arms. "Maybe not, but tell me this: If someone was in this room, how did they get in or out? There's only one door, and like Nancy said, it was locked from the inside. And you were at the door right after you heard Charlotte scream, so there was no time for someone to leave the room, right?"

I nodded.

"And take a look at this window," George went on. "It's a straight fifteen-foot drop down. No one would have climbed out of here to escape."

I had to admit, George had a point. "That's true," I replied, "but it all assumes that Charlotte did actually see someone in her room. It's possible that it was just a shadow, or a trick of the light."

"I guess so," George said, shrugging. "But I still prefer my ghost story."

The doctor spoke up behind us, and we all turned around. "Well, Charlotte," he said, "it looks like you're no worse for wear. Just take a couple aspirin for the pain and get some rest. You should be fine in the morning."

"Thanks, Uncle Harry," Charlotte said as he left. She looked around at the people gathered in the room and gave a nervous laugh. "Well," she said, "this isn't quite the way I envisioned my wedding preparations to begin."

"We'll get to the bottom of this, Charlotte," I found myself saying. "Don't worry."

Piper regarded me with interest. "You know," she said, "with all the commotion, I don't think we've been properly introduced. I'm Piper, Charlotte's older sister and her maid of honor."

Charlotte made the introductions, including Bess and George as well. The young man named Morgan stepped up and shook everyone's hands—including Charlotte's. "It's a pleasure to meet you," Morgan told her. "I've heard so much about you."

Charlotte smiled awkwardly and shot Piper a look. "I wish I could say the same—sis, I didn't know you were bringing a plus one."

Piper slapped her head in dismay. "Oh jeez, Char, I'm so sorry! Morgan and I started dating a while back—I must have been so caught up in our time together that I totally forgot to ask you to add him to the guest list."

Charlotte looked at the two of them—their arms linked together, bodies pressed close—and sighed.

"I guess it's not a big deal," she finally said. "I can squeeze him in at the bridal party's table at the reception."

"You're the best, Char," Piper said with a winning smile. Then her eyes zeroed in on something behind Charlotte. "Is that the dress?!" she exclaimed, and dashed over to the white gown hanging on the bathroom door. "Ohh," she breathed, running her fingers over the creamy, beaded satin. "It's gorgeous."

"I just hope I can pull it off," Charlotte said wearily. "Mrs. Hill insisted I wear something . . . extravagant. She had her heart set on a big Southern wedding. Honestly, the thing would look much better on you." She turned to the girls and me. "I don't know if Piper mentioned this, but she's been modeling since she was a kid," she explained.

"Oh, pish," Piper replied gaily, waving us off. "It's just a few jobs here and there. Pays the bills. And anyway"—her eyes returned to her sister—"you're the one marrying the famous news anchor!"

"I am, aren't I," Charlotte murmured. All of a sudden, she looked terribly drained.

"Well," I announced to the room. "Charlotte, unless there's anything else you need, I think we should all let you rest. Doctor's orders."

We were all trooping out of the room when Charlotte said, "Wait!" We turned around, and Charlotte regarded us seriously. "Whatever you do, please keep this between us. You've seen how superstitious Mrs. Hill is, and she's been helping me organize this wedding for months. If she catches wind of something strange happening . . ." Her voice trailed off. "Well, I just don't want to find out how she's going to react."

"We won't say a word," Bess promised. We all nodded in agreement. Charlotte looked a little relieved, and we left her sitting on the bed and closed the door softly behind us.

"There's a cocktail hour with appetizers and things being served downstairs," Piper told us. "You girls should come and enjoy yourselves!"

"Thanks—we'll be down in a minute," Bess said.

"Sure thing!" Piper said with a smile, and then she and Morgan headed downstairs.

"I never would have guessed that those two were sisters!" I said once they were out of earshot. "They couldn't be more different if they tried."

Bess nodded. "They've always been like that, ever since they were little. I always had a closer relationship with Charlotte."

"I guess opposites really do attract," George added.

"Clearly," I chuckled. "Look at the two of you!"

Bess smirked. "Well, yes. But it was never really that way with Charlotte and Piper. Piper was always in the spotlight, always getting all the attention from kids at school—especially boys. On the other hand, Charlotte was quiet and bookish—she kept to herself most of the time, and only had a few really close friends. Honestly, I'm a little surprised that Charlotte asked her to be the maid of honor." After a moment, Bess shrugged. "Though I guess it makes sense. They are sisters. And it certainly seems like they've overcome whatever differences they had when they were younger."

"Enough gossip," George said, clapping her hands. "Time to eat!"

Back downstairs, the main room had filled up with the last members of the bridal party and their families who had arrived from out of town. The sun was setting, casting the room in a warm, pinkish light. Tables of finger food and drinks had been set out, and George's eyes lit up when she saw them. "Thank goodness," she said, grabbing a small plate and piling it with cheese and rolls of deli meat. "I'm famished! We haven't had a bite since those measly snacks on the plane. Maybe this can be our dinner!"

After picking up some fruit and crudités, I stepped up to the drinks table to pour myself some lemonade. Parker was already there, filling up his own glass with sweet tea. I considered telling him what had happened to Charlotte, but thought better of it—she might want to explain the situation to him herself. Parker was about to step away when a small, older woman in a lavender floral dress stopped him. "Oh my gracious," she said in a tremulous voice. "You are even more handsome in person than you are on TV!"

Parker must have been used to this kind of thing, because he didn't even blush. "Why, that's most kind of you to say, ma'am," he replied smoothly. "Are you a friend of the family?"

"I used to play bridge with your mother in the old days," the woman replied. "Now, would you make an old lady's week, young man, and take a picture with me?"

"It would be my pleasure," Parker said.

The woman unceremoniously pushed a blocky old digital camera into my hands before cozying up to Parker. "Just push the button at the top," she ordered.

I obeyed, and the flash fluttered in their eyes before capturing the image. I handed the camera back to the woman, who immediately squinted at the display to make sure I had taken a satisfactory photo. "Thank you, dear," she said to Parker, pumping his hand and then hurrying away.

Parker met my eyes, his own sparkling with good

humor. "You've got to give the people what they want," he said with a smile. A moment later he was called across the room by his father and gave me a quick wave before walking away.

"Some guys have all the luck," said a voice. I turned to see an angular young man standing nearby, leaning against the back of a couch with a cup of coffee grasped in one hand. He had a mop of curly brown hair on his head and was wearing a white button-down shirt with the sleeves rolled up.

"What do you mean?" I asked.

"Parker. He's good-looking, successful, wealthy—and now he's marrying some Harvard-educated gal with enough brains to fill a football stadium!" He shook his head in wonder, watching the groom-to-be greeting guests across the crowded room. "The guy's got good luck coming out of his ears, that's all I'm saying." He looked over at me, as if waking up from a dream. "Oh, boy—have I been running my mouth off again? Sorry! The name's Tucker Matthews. I'm Parker's coworker and one of the groomsmen."

"Nancy Drew," I said with a smile.

"Hope to see you around, Nancy Drew," Tucker said, and raised his coffee in a toast. "Here's to some good luck for the rest of us."

I left Tucker at the drinks table and wound my way through the crowd until I found Bess and George. "I'm beat," I told them. "It's been a long day, so I think I'm going to head up to my room and go to bed."

"I'm going to stay up a while longer," Bess said. "The bridesmaids are all planning to discuss the plans for the next couple days—there's a lot still to do!"

"I'll come with you," George said to me. "Just let me grab one more plate of food for the road."

After George gathered up a towering pile of cookies and pastries, we both headed up the spiral staircase to our rooms. I managed a good night as we parted, my feet feeling heavier with every step. I could hardly wait to get into my pajamas and between the sheets.

I slipped into my cozy room, changed my clothes, brushed my teeth, and crawled gratefully into bed. I thought that the events of the evening might keep me awake, despite how tired I was, but I was wrong. I was out cold as soon as my head hit the pillow.

It felt like only minutes had passed when I woke up with a start. I glanced over at the digital clock I had placed on the nightstand; it read 3:19 a.m. I had been fast asleep for hours—what had woken me up? I raised my head to look around the room, and my heart leaped into my throat.

There, standing at the foot of my bed, was a figure, looming in the darkness.

CHAPTER THREE

Night Terrors

WITH A STARTLED CRY, I LEAPED OUT OF bed and tried to get a better look at the intruder. With only the moonlight streaming in from the window, it was hard to make out any details—but just as Charlotte had said, it appeared that the figure was dressed in some sort of uniform. Both jacket and pants were of a single color—blue, perhaps?—and the coat's metal buttons flashed in the dim light.

"Don't come any closer," I warned, trying to keep my voice from shaking. I scanned the room for something I could use as a weapon and landed on a heavy-looking crystal vase on the nightstand by my side. I grabbed it by the neck and whirled back around to face the intruder—

But he was gone.

Shaken, I darted across the room to the lamp on the dresser and switched it on. Yellow light flooded the room, revealing no one but my own pale reflection in the vanity mirror. I quickly checked the closet and bathroom, but to no avail. Whoever had been in my room had vanished. But how?

The door was chained and bolted; the windows, too. Curious, I unlocked the door and stepped out into the dark hallway, searching for any sign of movement. A single candle was burning on a table near my door, casting eerie shadows on the wall. I picked it up by the metal candlestick and raised it in front of me, casting my gaze around, looking for any sign of movement. A second later, I heard the telltale groan of an old floorboard and ran out to the main hallway to see who was there.

"Gah!" George yelped, sloshing the drink in her

hand down the front of her T-shirt. "You scared the daylights out of me, Nancy!" She brushed at the wetness spreading across her shirt and asked, "Did you get thirsty too? I think there's some more lemonade downstairs. . . ." Her words died as she saw the expression on my face. "Uh, Nance? Is everything okay? You look like you've seen a—"

"He was there," I interrupted, leaning back against the bookcases for support. My heart was racing. "In my room. Just like Charlotte said. I don't understand it, but I—"

"Whoa, whoa, whoa," George said, raising her hands. "Take it easy. Let's go back to your room; you can explain everything. And here"—she handed me her glass of lemonade—"I think you need this more than I do."

Setting the candle back on the table in the hallway, we returned to my room. Once we had settled down, I went through everything that happened with George. The sighting was virtually identical to Charlotte's account, and I felt sheepish for doubting her. But that still left the question: If we weren't dealing with a rambunctious ghost, how was this person getting in and out of the rooms? And more importantly: What did they want?

As I spoke, George paced the room, her eyebrows knitted in thought. Suddenly she stopped midstep and knelt down to inspect something at her feet. "What's this?" she asked.

I walked over to her and saw that she had found a scattering of gray-brown dust on the floor near one wall. It was arranged in a jagged line, as if it had fallen from something as it passed by. I touched some of it and raised my finger to my nose. It smelled of earth and smoke. "Ash," I said with certainty. "But it's the height of summer! No one's using the inn's fireplaces now. Where could it have come from?"

George shook her head, puzzled. "No idea. But it's the only clue we've got."

I sat back on my heels, a familiar feeling tingling in my gut.

"You think there's a mystery afoot?" George asked, her eyes on mine.

"I don't know—yet," I answered. "But there's no denying that something strange is going on."

George nodded, and yawned hugely. "Well, whatever it is, I think it can wait until morning," she said sleepily.

"Yes," I agreed, yawning back at her. "Good night, then."

After George went back to her room, I locked and bolted the door once more, but realized that doing so was a futile gesture. If something wanted to get in, I didn't know how to stop it.

Needless to say, it took quite a while for me to get back to sleep.

The next time I woke up, the room was bathed in sunlight, which made the events of the night before feel almost like a dream. I was brushing my teeth when I first heard the sound of many voices filtering up from the floor below. When I looked at my clock, I saw that it was only seven thirty in the morning; what could possibly have that many people up and chattering at this early hour?

Ten minutes later I walked down the spiral staircase to find many of the same guests from last night's gathering back in the main room, talking animatedly among themselves.

"It was the darnedest thing," I heard one woman say. "The door just slammed, all by itself!"

"A whole shelf's worth of books fell to the floor," a man nearby exclaimed. "Right in front of my eyes!"

The elderly woman who had asked for Parker's picture was shaking her head somberly in reaction to some other tale of supernatural happenings from last night. "The out-of-towners might deny it," she said with a knowing tone. "But any Charleston native knows that this old place has more ghosts than a Halloween fun house!"

A moment later Bess and George appeared next to me, Bess looking much more rested than both George and I did. "Well," I told them, "it looks like I wasn't the only one to have a visitor last night. Everyone seems to have a story of their own!"

John William, the owner of the inn, was surrounded

by a throng of people, regaling them with stories about the inn's ghosts. Some of Parker's friends from the news were among them, scribbling into slim notebooks.

"The Grey Fox hasn't seen paranormal activity on this scale in decades," he said. "It's almost unprecedented. Perhaps the ghosts wanted to be a part of the wedding of the year too!" A few people tittered at the joke, and one of the reporters pushed through to the front, asking John William some more questions.

Bess nudged me, nodding her head toward the other side of the room, where Mrs. Hill stood with her husband behind the breakfast table, dabbing at her temples with a silk handkerchief. She looked pale and distraught, her eyes rimmed with red. "Looks like not everyone is enjoying the ghosts as much as John William is," Bess noted.

I nodded. Mrs. Hill was murmuring something to her husband, but I couldn't hear what she was saying. Curious, I told the girls I wanted to pick up a few croissants and some juice and made my way over to where they were standing.

"What are we going to do, Cash?" I heard Mrs. Hill say as I neared. "I thought we were doing good by our boy by picking this place, and now look what's happened. This dignified ceremony is turning into some kind of dog and pony show!" She shuddered. "What if this is a bad omen?"

I winced. It looked like Charlotte's hope to keep all this a secret had been short-lived.

"Come on now, sugar, be reasonable," Mr. Hill replied. "A few little spooks and specters aren't gonna ruin our boy's big day. Everything's going to be fine."

"We should have stayed at the Palmetto Inn," Mrs. Hill said, loud enough for everyone around the table to hear. "I knew there was a reason this place had so many vacancies at the height of wedding season, and now we know what it is." Then Mr. Hill whisked his wife away, muttering something about last-minute table adjustments for the reception.

Next to me, I saw Charlotte's mother pouring herself a cup of coffee, with Mr. Goodwin standing next to her, a steaming mug already in his hands. He was staring after the Hills, shaking his head in obvious irritation. "If she wanted the Palmetto Inn," he muttered to Mrs. Goodwin, "they could have paid for it themselves. We would have had to take out a second mortgage on the house to pay for that place."

"Russell!" Mrs. Goodwin admonished him, her eyes scanning the room. "Keep your voice down, will you?" She caught me watching them before I could avert my gaze. "Oh, good morning—Nancy, is it? I hope you got more rest last night than the rest of us!"

"Actually . . . ," I started to say, but my voice trailed off when I saw Charlotte standing across the room. She must have just come downstairs. She was surrounded by a group of guests who—from the look of panic spreading over her face—were probably filling her in on the evening's many hauntings. "Excuse me, Mrs. Goodwin, I'm going to go see if Charlotte needs anything."

As I made my way across the room, I saw that George and Bess had had the same idea and were already at Charlotte's side. "Sorry, everyone!" Bess called out to the group of guests. "I'm going to have to steal the beautiful bride for a bit—lots to do today!" And with that, Bess smoothly ushered Charlotte out of the main room and onto the front patio.

"Thank you so much," Charlotte said to Bess as soon as the door closed behind us. "I don't know how much longer I could have lasted in there. Between my parents and Parker's parents being at each other's throats, and all these ghost sightings last night"—she plopped heavily into a wicker rocking chair—"this wedding is turning out to be a complete disaster."

"Don't be silly," Bess said. "These kinds of problems always happen at weddings. Don't you remember Aunt Jessica and Uncle John's wedding? How the product they used in Aunt Jess's hair attracted a whole hive full of bees right in the middle of the ceremony? Well, they still had a lovely wedding and are happily married—despite a few little stings! Right?" She patted Charlotte's arm. "Let's focus on getting things done. What do you need to do this morning?"

Charlotte nodded. "You're right. Worrying doesn't

help. Well, we need to go drop off something at the bakery making the cakes, and a check for the florist as well."

"Not a moment to waste, then!" Bess said. "Let's go, ladies!"

A little while later, we arrived at the Sugar & Spice Bakery, a tiny boutique with powder-blue and cotton-candy-pink decor. A cloud of warm, sweet-smelling air greeted us the moment we walked through the door, and my mouth instantly started to water. I was starving—I had been so caught up in eavesdropping that I hadn't gotten a bite to eat back at the inn. A larger-than-life woman emerged from the back—she wore a white apron, and her hands were covered with a thin layer of flour. "Well, hello, honey!" she boomed at the sight of Charlotte. "Oh, I see you brought some friends today!"

"Hi, Carla," Charlotte said. It was the first time I'd seen her smile today.

"Come on inside, everybody," Carla said, ushering

us farther in with a wave of her enormous arm. "I just pulled a tray of blackberry muffins from the oven—y'all can be my guinea pigs."

And before I knew it, a warm muffin oozing with blackberry juice was stuffed into my hands. I took a bite and groaned. "This is the best thing I've ever eaten," I said through a mouthful.

Carla hooted with laughter. "Girl, you're just trying to get on my good side, ain't you?" She turned to Charlotte. "Now, honey, have you brought them?"

Charlotte rifled through her purse until she found a small white box. When she opened it, I saw four silver charms inside, each one with a white ribbon tied to it. She handed the box to Carla. "What are those for?" George asked.

"It's part of a Southern wedding tradition," Charlotte explained, "called a charm cake. In addition to the wedding cake, the couple has a second cake made with different charms baked between the layers. The ribbons are left trailing out. During the reception, each of the bridesmaids and the maid of honor chooses a ribbon and pulls out the charm. The charms all have different meanings."

"Kind of like a fortune cookie," George said.

Charlotte nodded.

"Speaking of charm," Carla said, leaning across the counter, "how about you tell that charming fiancé of yours to do a local interest story about a very special bakery right here in downtown Charleston?"

Charlotte chuckled. "For you, Carla—anything," she said.

"Ooh, sugar," Carla hummed with a blinding smile, "I'm going to bake you a cake you are never going to forget!"

Next we made our way to the florist, which was only a few blocks away. The shop was bustling with employees rushing in and out with bundles of flowers, while a tall, reedy man barked orders at them from behind a desk. "The lilies are for the Rogers/Flynn wedding, not the Thompson funeral! And get those orchids on ice before they wilt!"

"I'm sorry to bother you," Charlotte said, walking

up to him. "But I've just come to drop off a check for the remainder of my order."

"It's not a bother, my dear," the man said, dabbing at his forehead with a handkerchief. "It's always like this in the late summer months. Everyone is either getting married or dying, all at the same time." He took the check from her hand and squinted at it. "Hmm," he muttered, and tapped at the keys of his laptop.

"Is something wrong?" Charlotte asked.

"Ah, yes," the man said, looking at the screen. "I'm sorry, miss, but this isn't enough to cover the cost."

Charlotte looked perplexed. "I don't understand. I called just last week, and this was the figure you quoted me."

The man nodded. "Yes, but that was before you changed the rose color from white to yellow. We don't get a lot of demand for yellow roses, so I had to have them custom ordered."

Charlotte had gone pale. "Changed the color? But—but I never did that."

"You must be mistaken, miss," the man replied. "I got

a call from you just yesterday, making that specific request. I thought it was strange myself, given what most people think about yellow roses, but I figured, to each his own."

Charlotte had her head in her hands. I turned to her and asked, "Why would someone impersonate you just to change the color of your roses? It doesn't make any sense."

"And what's so wrong with yellow roses, anyway?" Bess asked.

Charlotte looked up at us with tears in her eyes. "Yellow roses have always been seen as bad luck. They represent jealousy and . . . infidelity." She spoke the last word as if it were a curse. Then she looked at me, with a wild desperation in her eyes. "Nancy, maybe this is crazy, but it feels like someone is trying to ruin my wedding."

I thought about everything that had happened since we'd arrived at the Grey Fox Inn, and I knew that my earlier instincts had been correct. "I don't think you're crazy, Charlotte," I said. "I think you're right. And I promise, I'm going to get to the bottom of it."

CHAPTER FOUR

Practice Makes Perfect

CHARLOTTE HAD TO GO TAKE CARE OF some details for the rehearsal dinner that night, so we dropped her off back at the inn before heading back out to do a little sightseeing and last-minute shopping for the wedding. It was late afternoon and blazing hot once the girls and I got back to the inn. We all guzzled several glasses of complimentary iced tea before heading upstairs, sweaty and tired.

George and I followed Bess into her room to talk.

"For a while there, I thought my face was on fire," said George, collapsing on the bed. "It took all my willpower not to pour that whole pitcher of tea right on top of my head!"

Bess sighed. "I just hope this heat doesn't make my hair all pouffy," she said, fanning herself with a travel magazine. "That is just the worst."

"Not worse than having some loony sabotaging your wedding," George muttered. She craned her head to look at me. "So, detective, what's the plan?"

I took a deep breath and began pacing the room. "Well, we don't know for sure if the incidents here at the inn and the change in the flowers are related. It makes sense that they are, but we can't assume anything yet. If this person is looking to disrupt Charlotte's wedding, these events might only be the beginning."

Bess perched on one of the armchairs near the bed. "But who would want to ruin the wedding? Charlotte is such a nice girl. . . . I can't imagine anyone wanting to hurt her."

"Well, if we've learned anything from all our cases," I said, "it's that anyone can make enemies. Even if someone wasn't trying to hurt Charlotte, they might have another reason they'd want to stop the wedding."

"And Charlotte isn't necessarily the target," George added. "It's just as likely that Parker is the intended victim—it's his wedding too, after all."

I nodded. "We need to start building a list of suspects. The culprit is probably staying at the inn, someone close to the action. They'd need to know where and when everything is happening, and be able to create these disruptions without attracting attention to themselves."

"But everyone at the inn is either friends or family," Bess said.

I shrugged, apologetic. "Sorry, Bess, but many crimes are committed by people close to the victim." When Bess looked stricken, I laid my hand on her shoulder. "Don't worry—we'll stop this person before they can mess up Charlotte's big day."

Bess nodded. "Okay, so who's on the list?"

"Well, I hate to say it," George began, "but I think Mr. Goodwin should be on it."

"Charlotte's dad?!" Bess spluttered. "But why would Uncle Russ want to stop the wedding?"

I tapped my chin thoughtfully. "It's a long shot—but for now, I agree with you, George. Mr. Goodwin has made it pretty clear he's unhappy about how much money he's spending on this event, and it seems like he blames Parker's parents for it."

"It is very traditional that the bride's family pay for the majority of the cost," Bess agreed. "And Uncle Russ is a lot more forward-thinking than the Hills seem to be, so he probably didn't appreciate their 'tradition' very much. But you really think he'd do this to his own daughter, just over money?"

"If Mr. Goodwin doesn't like the family Charlotte's marrying into, he might be willing to go pretty far to put a stop to the wedding," George reasoned.

"Okay, fine," Bess said, sighing. "He's on the list—for now."

"The only other person I can add is a guy named

Tucker Matthews," I said. "I met him last night; he's one of the groomsmen. He seemed a little envious of Parker's luck—his career, his marriage, everything. It's not much to go on, but he's the only other person so far who has any motive."

"Well, like you said," George remarked, getting up and stretching, "it's only the beginning."

A moment later there was a knock at the door. I opened it to find Charlotte's sister, Piper, standing in the hallway, looking even more luminous than before in a floral sundress and wide-brimmed hat. "I hope I'm not interrupting anything," she said with an apologetic smile. "But I just wanted to remind you and your friends that the bridal party will be leaving for the rehearsal in an hour. It's at Our Lady of Truth on Broad Street."

"Of course!" I said. "I must have lost track of time. We'll be there." After closing the door, I turned back to Bess and George. "We'll have to leave the rest of the sleuthing for later—we've all got to get dressed for the rehearsal!"

After agreeing to meet Bess and George down in

the main room in forty-five minutes, I walked down the hall back toward my room. A young maid, with her black hair tied up in a bun, stood in the hallway with her cleaning cart, wrangling a large bag of linens into place. Her name tag read ANNABELLE. I walked past her to my room and began rummaging in my purse for the room key. Out of the corner of my eye, I saw Piper and Morgan coming down the hallway and stopping a few doors down at what I guessed was their room. Then I heard Annabelle say, "Excuse me, sir, but haven't we met before?"

I looked up, curious. Morgan was staring at the maid, startled. Piper looked at Annabelle, then back at Morgan, and for a moment an angry expression crossed her face. But she quickly masked it and said, in a convincingly pleasant voice, "I'm sorry, miss, but you must be mistaken. Now, we're very busy. If you could come back later to make up the beds, I'd appreciate it." And without waiting for an answer, she and Morgan walked into the room and shut the door behind them. Annabelle stared at the closed door for a few seconds before turning back to her work.

Strange, I thought as I unlocked my room. Though, from the looks of Morgan, he seemed like the kind of guy who probably dated a lot of women. If Annabelle had known Morgan in the past, that would explain Piper's reaction to her. As I pulled out the summery aqua-and-coral-striped gown I'd brought for the rehearsal that night, I wondered what other strange things the evening might bring.

Our Lady of Truth was a beautiful old church right in the heart of historic Charleston. Palm trees clustered beneath its creamy-white bell tower, which gleamed in the late afternoon sun. It was blissfully cool inside, and the clacking of my heels on the marble floor echoed through the massive nave, with its soaring ceiling and ornate stained-glass windows. Bess, George, and I walked down the central aisle to join the bridesmaids and groomsmen who were already gathered at the front of the church. The Goodwins were seated on one side of the pews, the Hills on the other—which is tradition, but it made the emotional distance between them seem like a physical reality. Charlotte and Parker were up at the altar, speaking to the reverend who would be officiating the ceremony.

While Bess dragged George off to meet some of the family, I hung back, admiring the beauty of the church. "It's almost three hundred years old, you know," a voice behind me said. I turned to see a petite, full-figured young woman with ebony skin standing there. She was wearing a sleeveless navy dress and wore small, silver-rimmed glasses.

"Oh, really?" I replied, interested.

"Yes, it's one of the oldest structures in Charleston, actually." She was about to continue when she stopped herself, embarrassed. "Look at me, spouting on about history without even introducing myself. I'm Alicia, one of the bridesmaids." She held out her hand.

She had a very firm handshake for such a small person, and I returned it as best I could. "I'm Nancy, a friend of Charlotte's cousin Bess. And how do you know Charlotte?"

"We studied history together in college," Alicia

replied. "Roommates for four years!" She shook her head and chuckled. "We probably drank enough coffee to fill the Colosseum. But we had a good time, Char and I. We were such nerds. . . . We always thought that we'd end up being dusty old cat ladies together, still sticking our noses in books all day." Alicia's eyes lit upon Charlotte standing on the altar—she appeared much more relaxed than earlier and looked lovely in her lacy, plum-colored dress. "I never expected either of us to end up like this," Alicia finished.

I watched Alicia's face with interest; she seemed fond of Charlotte, but there was also a twinge of resentment in her voice. "I guess you never know what the future will hold," I said, keeping the tone light.

"It's funny," Alicia went on dreamily. "If things had gone a little differently, it might have been me up there. Charlotte and I were both doing an internship at the Charleston Historical Society when our friend Reggie—he's the best man—introduced her to Parker. I just happened to be out sick that day. I remember she had her first date with him the same day she found out she was awarded the grant we had both applied for. Quite an impressive run for Charlotte."

"I'm . . . sorry," I said, a little awkwardly.

Alicia chuckled to herself. "Don't be sorry. After all that, I ended up leaving Charleston for a new life in Florida. All's well that ends well. Anyway, it looks like the rehearsal's starting!"

Despite her reassurances, I wasn't totally convinced that Alicia didn't hold a grudge against Charlotte for getting the guy and the grant. Given how close they had been, it wasn't too hard to imagine that Alicia would like to see Charlotte's marriage fall through. Alicia's envy put her onto my list of suspects—right next to Tucker Matthews.

From the altar, the reverend was calling for everyone to gather together to practice the procession. "If you aren't in the bridal party, please take a seat!" he said. "Bridesmaids and groomsmen, pair up with your assigned partners at the foot of the aisle. Charlotte will put you in the right order."

I sat down with George in one of the front pews

while Bess linked arms with one of Parker's handsome cousins and made her way to the back of the church. "Check out that guy's face," George said. "He looks like he just won the lottery."

I grinned. "Well, Bess is quite a catch."

Right before the procession was about to start, I saw Mrs. Hill get up from her seat, rush over to the reverend, and whisper something in his ear. The reverend's eyebrows shot up, but after a moment he nodded and called out, "Excuse me, Charlotte—Mrs. Hill is a little concerned about you participating in the processional yourself. She believes . . . well, that it's bad luck for the bride to walk down the aisle before her wedding day."

There was a pregnant silence before Charlotte replied, "Is it, now?"

The reverend cleared his throat uncomfortably. "Apparently so."

Charlotte walked back up to the altar, carefully composing herself as she went. "Then I suppose I'll need a stand-in."

"I'll do it!" Piper called out from where she was standing with Reggie, the best man.

Mrs. Hill leaned over to the reverend again and whispered something else in his ear. "Ah, Mrs. Hill thinks it might be better if it's someone unrelated to the family," he said.

Charlotte turned to face Piper. "It's okay, sis. Anyway, I need you to walk with Reggie so it's just like the real thing. Thanks, though."

Piper shrugged. "Just trying to help!" she said sweetly.

"How about Nancy?" Bess said. "She's not related."

I froze in my seat. Me? A stand-in for the bride?

"You mean the redhead?" Mrs. Hill said, forgetting to whisper into the reverend's ear again. Apparently the mother of the groom hadn't forgotten that I was a walking, talking bad-luck charm.

"Mother . . . ," I heard Parker growl.

Mrs. Hill recovered quickly and smiled at me. "If you're willing, Miss Drew. I would . . . very much appreciate it."

"Sure, of course," I said, trying to sound breezy. Truthfully, I felt like my knees had turned to water. I may not blink an eye at facing down criminals or running full tilt into danger—but standing up in front of a lot of people? People who are looking at me? I'd take a high-speed car chase over that any day.

Despite my fear, I stood up and walked down the aisle to where the rest of the bridal party was lined up and took my place last in line, where the bride was supposed to stand. Bess grinned back at me. "How could you do this to me?" I grumbled.

"Lighten up, Nancy," she said with a giggle. "This will be fun. Oh! I almost forgot!" She grabbed a bag sitting on the floor nearby and pulled out a bouquet made of gift bows and a plain white veil. "These are from the bridal shower Charlotte had a few weeks ago. It's tradition for the bride to wear them during the rehearsal. And today, that's you!"

Before I could protest, Bess had pinned the veil to the top of my head and shoved the bow bouquet into my hands. "I feel ridiculous," I said.

"You're cute as a button!" Bess said, snapping a picture with her phone. "Now get ready, we're about to walk in!"

One by one, each couple walked down the aisle as romantic piano music was piped in through the speaker system. Finally it was down to me. I took a deep breath, prayed that I wouldn't trip over my own feet, and started down the aisle.

As I went, painfully slowly to match the music, I felt every eye in the entire church on me. I looked around the room and thought that one of these people was probably the person responsible for sabotaging Charlotte's wedding. But who?

I finally got up to the front and passed the pew where George was sitting. She leaned over and whispered, loud enough for me to hear, "Looking good, Nance—that veil was made for you!"

Blushing, I nudged George with my foot—hard— as I went by. If only Ned could see me now!

CHAPTER FIVE

Danger at Dinner

AFTER TWO MORE PRACTICE RUNS OF THE procession and the recession, the rehearsal was over. George chortled gleefully at the dozens of embarrassing pictures she had taken with her phone. "Look at your face!" she giggled, showing me a snapshot of myself cowering under the gauzy veil. "You look like you'd rather be getting a root canal."

"Humph," I grumbled. "Well, it isn't far from the truth."

"These are going straight to Ned!" she announced, tapping at the screen.

"Don't you dare!" I lunged for the phone, laughing, just as Bess walked up.

"Oh, calm down, Nancy," she said, smiling. "Just because Ned sees you wearing a wedding veil doesn't mean it will send him running for the hills."

I chuckled. "I suppose not."

"Anyway, everyone's heading over to Indigo Blue for dinner—here are the directions." Bess handed me a slip of paper with detailed directions to the restaurant—complete with map and points of interest on the way.

"Charlotte strikes again," I said, impressed at the level of detail. "She really does think of everything."

"Everything except why someone would want to mess up her wedding," George muttered. "Maybe we'll be able to gather more information at the rehearsal dinner."

"Let's hope so," I replied. "The wedding is tomorrow afternoon! And I have a feeling whoever is behind the pranks is planning something . . . tonight."

"I hope you're wrong," Bess said, her eyebrows creased with worry.

We made our way out of the church with the rest of the bridal party, jumped into the convertible, and followed the directions to the Indigo Blue restaurant a few miles away.

Indigo Blue was a sleek, modern building with huge windows on each side. The restaurant was perched right on the waterfront, overlooking the Ashley River, where a glorious pink-and-orange sunset burned on the horizon. A very well-dressed gentleman greeted us at the door and graciously led us in once we told him we were with the Goodwin-Hill wedding party.

"Wow, swanky," George said. "I bet the steaks here cost more than my car."

Bess snorted. "I bet the contents of my purse cost more than your car."

George stopped, hands on hips. "And what is that supposed to mean?"

Bess smirked. "It means you need a new car."

While George tried to defend her car—which, by the way, is held together with duct tape and a prayer—we all walked into the main dining room, where guests were already milling about, drinking cocktails and munching on appetizers. After finding our names on a seating list, we discovered that Bess would be sitting up front with the rest of the bridesmaids and grooms-men, while George and I would be at a table with some of Parker's coworkers from the news station.

Since we were among the last guests to arrive, the waiters called everyone to their tables shortly after we located our seats. The tables were all adorned with tall vases full of white magnolias, and their sweet smell perfumed the air. The guests were bubbling with excitement, many of them exclaiming to one another about how delighted they were to be invited to Charleston's most anticipated wedding of the year. George and I sat down between a young blond woman and a stocky, middle-aged lady with iron-gray hair.

"Wow! I love your dress," the blonde exclaimed as we took our seats.

George didn't seem to register this, so I nudged her. "She's talking to you," I whispered.

"Me?!" George replied. She looked down in confusion at her army-green asymmetrical shift dress. "You really like it?"

"Oh, yeah. It's really contemporary—gritty. I think I saw something just like it on the runway last month! You're, like, ahead of the trend."

"Um, cool," George said, blushing. Being fashionable wasn't normally part of George's wheelhouse, but I could tell she was tickled by the compliment. "I'm George, by the way, and this is Nancy. We're friends of the bride."

"I'm Marsha," the blonde said. "I'm one of the production assistants at WCHR—my job is to make Parker look good." She winked.

I looked over at Parker, who was greeting groups at each table and looked like a million dollars in his light-gray suit. "I know what you're thinking," Marsha continued. "Making Parker Hill look good can't be very hard. Well, you're right. Of all the anchors I've had to work with, Parker is the best by a mile. The guy hasn't a mean bone in his body."

It was nice to hear, but part of me grumbled at this. A really nice guy doesn't have a lot of enemies—which made for a very short list of suspects. I decided to dig a little deeper. "And how about Tucker Matthews?" I asked. "I met him at the inn yesterday, and he seemed like a nice guy. Do you work with him, too?"

Marsha glanced across the table at the middle-aged woman, and when she saw that the woman was deep in conversation with another guest, Marsha lowered her voice and moved in close. "Well, I don't like to gossip, especially not with our boss listening"—she nodded toward the middle-aged woman—"but Tucker has not been doing well lately. I used to work with him on the morning broadcast, but then he and Parker started vying for the open anchor position on the evening news. Obviously, Parker got the gig. The executives decided to put Tucker on at midnight, since it was the only other anchor position open, and they needed someone to do it. Tucker put a good face on it and all, but everyone knows he's unhappy. It was a real blow."

I nodded thoughtfully. "But there was no bad blood between Tucker and Parker after that?"

Marsha shrugged. "Tucker's in this wedding, isn't he? I guess maybe he's decided to let bygones be bygones."

Soon waiters appeared with plates of salad and baskets of warm rolls, and we all settled in to eat. Casually, I leaned over to George. "Well, what do you think?" I asked.

George swallowed a mouthful of bread and said, "I think Tucker has the strongest motive we've seen so far. If Parker messed up his dream of being a popular anchor, then why not mess up Parker's dream wedding as retribution?"

I pondered this as I speared a cucumber. "He's definitely one to watch," I said. "But let's see how the rest of the night plays out."

As I finished crunching my salad, I overheard a woman at the table behind me speaking in a loud voice.

"I'm missing my favorite gold chain-link bracelet. I

could have sworn I brought it with me, but I can't find it anywhere in my hotel room."

A man joked, "Maybe the ghost took it."

I had to solve this mystery, and fast!

Once the waiters whisked away the empty salad plates, I excused myself to the ladies' room. I followed the signs to a hallway off the dining room, but before I could reach the restroom, two familiar voices filled my ears.

"Stop this, Russell!" a woman's voice said. "You're being unreasonable!"

I quieted my footsteps and continued down the hallway toward the sounds of the voices. They were coming from the coatroom. The door was ajar, just enough to allow the voices to be heard from where I stood, but not so far as to allow the people inside to see me. I lingered outside the door, waiting to hear more.

"I'm being unreasonable?" a man's voice retorted. "It's those Hills who are the difficult ones! I should never have let them convince me to pony up for all this. I mean, sure, they're paying for this rehearsal dinner—but tonight's little meal is nothing compared to the cost of the rest of this 'Wedding of the Year'! If they wanted to make such a big splash and invite half the city, they should have paid for it themselves!"

Russell and Sharon, I thought. *Those are Charlotte's parents in there!*

"What I understand," Mrs. Goodwin replied, furious, "is that three months ago, you had no problem with any of this! You barely even looked at those numbers before you signed the contracts for everything. And now, all of a sudden, we get to Charleston and you're acting like someone held a gun to your head and forced you to pay for a wedding!"

There was a long moment of silence before Mr. Goodwin said anything more. "I'm . . . I'm sorry."

I heard Mrs. Goodwin sigh. "Russell, is there something you aren't telling me?"

Another pause. "Last week," Mr. Goodwin finally said, "a few days before our flight . . . I lost big in the stock market. Big. The CEO is less than pleased about it—he thinks I should have seen it coming. At any rate, it's not looking good for me."

"Oh, honey," Mrs. Goodwin breathed. I heard the rustle of an embrace. "Why didn't you tell me?"

"I didn't want to ruin the wedding for you. You should be thinking about Charlotte right now, not worrying about our finances."

"Perhaps, but—"

Just then, a couple of the guests came down the hallway, laughing and talking loudly. Mr. and Mrs. Goodwin went silent, and a moment later, Mr. Goodwin opened the coatroom door to find me standing right beside it. He glanced at me uncertainly.

"Oh!" I said, "Sorry, I was looking for the ladies' room. I guess I picked the wrong door!"

Mr. Goodwin's face relaxed. "No problem, Nancy. It's just down there on the left."

"Thanks!" I said with a smile. And with that, I scooted down the hall and away.

I thought about the conversation as I reapplied my

lipstick in the restroom. Mr. Goodwin's motives to stop the wedding just didn't add up. Money did make people do crazy things, but most of the money would have already been spent by now, wouldn't it? And from the sound of it, Mr. Goodwin only wanted the best for Charlotte—even if it meant putting up with some irritating in-laws. His negative attitude could be explained away by this problem with his job, plain and simple. Bess was right—Mr. Goodwin didn't belong on our list of suspects, after all.

Feeling at loose ends with the case, I made my way back to the table. Part of the problem with this mystery was that the relationship between the incidents so far was unclear. Sneaking into people's rooms at night was creepy—but the perpetrator didn't steal anything or hurt anyone. So was their motive simply to frighten people? Changing the flowers felt more like a personal insult, a move meant to rattle Charlotte and make her feel uneasy about the wedding.

Thinking about it all, I started to become uneasy myself. I realized exactly why as I reached my seat: the two incidents felt like a prelude. The main event was still to come.

"Check it out!" George said with a grin. "Southern barbecue!"

Sure enough, a plate heaping with sweet-smelling pulled pork, blocks of corn bread, and green beans was waiting for me at my place. George dove right in, but I hesitated. There's nothing like waiting for a crime to happen to make me lose my appetite.

Ding! Ding! Ding!

I looked up from my half-eaten peach pie à la mode to see Reggie, a handsome young man with a shaved head and coppery-brown skin, standing at the main table, tapping a spoon against his champagne glass. "Can I have your attention, please?" he was saying. He continued until the chatter around the dining room died down. "Thank you," he said with a smile. He cleared his throat. "For those of you I haven't met, my name is Reggie Banks, and I'm Parker's best man. I know that I'm supposed to make my big speech at the reception tomorrow, but for a wedding like this one"—he gestured to the room, filled to the brim with guests—"let's just say that I needed a little rehearsing for that, too." The audience all chuckled appreciatively.

My eyes flitted over to Bess, who was watching Reggie with obvious interest. She noticed me looking at her and silently mouthed *Wow*, her eyebrows waggling. I chuckled to myself. Leave it to Bess to set her sights on one of the most gorgeous guys in the room.

"Parker and I met when we were barely out of diapers," Reggie continued. "And we've been making trouble together ever since. Throughout the years, Parker grew to be much more than just the boy next door—he became my best friend."

There was a chorus of *aww*s around the room.

"Parker always loved to one-up me when it came to kindnesses—whether it was climbing up that tree to get my model airplane, because he knew I was afraid of heights; or helping me get elected class president in high school; or even convincing me to ask that pretty girl out to senior prom. I never thought I'd be able to get you back, man—but when I introduced you to a girl named Charlotte at the historical society, I knew I had done it."

A wave of appreciative laughter, and some scattered applause, broke out. Charlotte blushed, and next to her, I saw Piper dabbing at her eyes with a handkerchief.

"So, on this momentous day, I'd like to raise my glass to you, Parker Hill"—everyone else raised their glasses in unison—"and say this: Buddy, we're even."

The room thundered with applause as the bridal party emptied their glasses, and Parker stood to pull Reggie into a brotherly embrace. I glanced over at George and spied her sniffling. "Why, Georgia Fayne," I said with a grin. "Are you crying?"

George looked at me in horror at the use of her real name and quickly rubbed her eyes with the back of her hand. "Course not!" she grumbled. "Just got a little pepper in there . . ."

Now that the speech was over, the guests got up to wander around the room and mingle. George and

I made our way through the crowd up to the main table, where Bess and Charlotte were chatting. "It was a lovely dinner," I told the bride.

"Do you think so?" Charlotte replied.

"Absolutely!" George said. "Especially the barbecue."

Just then a waiter approached the table with a small box wrapped in yellow paper and tied up with a bow. "Excuse me, miss," he said to Charlotte. "But this gift was left for you on the table up front."

Charlotte looked perplexed. "But the guests know to bring gifts to the reception tomorrow, not tonight. Who left it?"

The waiter shrugged and turned away to clear the table. Charlotte sighed. "Well, I suppose I'll just have to bring it back to the inn with me."

"Oh, why don't you open it now, sis?" Piper said, coming up from behind. "It's just one gift." Some of the bridesmaids spoke up in agreement.

"Fine, fine," Charlotte said, throwing her hands up in defeat. She loosed the ribbon from the box and tore through the paper. But when she pried open the flaps of the box and put her hand inside, I saw all the color drain from her face. "Oh my God," she cried, dropping the box onto the table as if it held a snake.

I leaped forward and looked into the box myself. My heart hammering, I grabbed a napkin and used it to reach inside and pull out a small hunting knife, its silver blade glinting sharply in the overhead lights. Tied onto the handle with a yellow ribbon was a message written in block letters.

It read: *It should have been me.*

CHAPTER SIX

~

Bad Luck Bride

"WHAT IS THAT?" A VOICE RANG OUT, AND
within seconds Parker had run up to the table and
grabbed the knife from my hands. He glanced at the
threatening note, and his face twisted in shock and
confusion. "This came as a gift? Who would do such
a thing?"

"I don't know yet," I said, keeping my voice calm.
The last thing I needed was for this to cause a major
scene at the rehearsal dinner. "But Parker, I need you
to put the knife down. The fewer people who touch it,
the better." I immediately thought to dust the knife for

fingerprints, but between Charlotte's prints and now Parker's, the chances of getting a clean fingerprint off the weapon were slim.

While George and Bess shuttled Charlotte off to the ladies' room to console her, I took the opportunity to inspect the evidence. The box had been beautifully wrapped; the paper was thick and expensive, and the bow had been tied expertly. The fact that the paper was yellow was also suspect; it seemed all too possible that the culprit was the same person who'd switched the flowers. There was something else, too—a faint aroma coming off the box. It was a pleasant scent, a little citrusy. Maybe the culprit used a cleaning solution to wipe any identifying marks from the knife before placing it in the box?

And what about the message? *It should have been me.* It seemed to suggest envy as a motive for disrupting the wedding—which made Tucker and Alicia prime suspects. Both had reasons to feel angry about Parker and Charlotte's run of good luck. They were both staying at the Grey Fox Inn, too, so they would have had ample opportunity to commit some of the nighttime terrors that had frightened all the guests last night. I wrinkled my nose in annoyance—I still hadn't figured out exactly how the culprit had been sneaking in and out of locked rooms. Oh well, one problem at a time! I made a note to myself to try and interrogate Tucker and Alicia further whenever I got the chance.

I turned the knife over with the napkin, being careful not to touch it, and sighed. The knife posed more questions than it answered. But one thing was for certain—the person behind all these stunts was far from finished. They were determined to ruin this wedding.

I found George and Bess with Charlotte in the ladies' room, and things didn't look good. Charlotte was leaning against the wall of sinks, and her face was wet with tears, mascara running down her cheeks in long black streaks. George and Bess whirled when the door opened, eyes wide, but they relaxed when they saw it was me.

"Oh, Nancy," Charlotte moaned, her voice trembling with sobs. "My wedding is doomed! I knew it was all too good to be true—someone like Parker falling for a boring bookworm like me. I was so naive!" She stopped to blow her nose in a tissue. "I knew something would get in the way, I just never thought it would be something like this!"

I moved next to her and laid a hand on her shoulder. "This has nothing to do with you being naive, or not being a good match with your fiancé," I said. "And none of it is your fault. Someone has some kind of grudge against you or Parker, and this is their way of expressing it. We just need to figure out who it is and stop them before tomorrow night."

Bess nodded. "Nancy's right, Char. There's no way we're going to let some chump mess up your big day. But . . ." Bess bit her lip, looking uncomfortable. "Do you know anyone who might feel that way? Someone who wishes they were the one getting married instead of you two?"

Charlotte wiped her eyes dry with a paper towel and

sniffed. "There are probably dozens of girls who wish they were marrying Parker instead of me—I mean, he's a local celebrity. But I can't think of anyone in particular. And as far as somebody wishing they were in Parker's shoes . . ." She shrugged. "I have no idea. I'm just a nearsighted history buff who would rather organize my book collection than spend a night out on the town. I don't exactly have a ton of experience with guys fighting over me."

George crossed her arms and suddenly looked fierce. "Listen here, Charlotte," she said sternly. "Don't ever sell yourself short like that! Any guy worth his salt would much rather end up with a girl with a brain and some passion than just another pretty face. And I bet that if you asked Parker, he'd say the same thing. I bet he'd say he's lucky to have someone like you."

Bess was beaming at George, a little teary-eyed herself. "George!" she exclaimed. "That is like . . . the sweetest thing you've ever said."

Charlotte managed a smile. "Thanks, George," she said quietly.

Outside the door, the sound of conversations had gotten louder. Something was going on back in the dining room. I turned back to the girls. "Listen, I think you two should just take Charlotte back to the inn—dinner is over anyway, and people will be leaving soon. The last thing Charlotte needs is to have to answer a bunch of questions about what happened. I'll grab the knife and the box and get it out of here before too many people can see it. Okay?"

Everyone agreed—Bess and George led Charlotte out a side door to the car, and I made my way back into the dining room, promising them that I'd explain the situation to Parker and hitch a ride back with someone.

Unfortunately, it was clear from the moment I got back in the room that it was already too late to conceal the knife from the other guests. Mrs. Hill was standing over the open gift box, gesticulating wildly, while Mr. Hill and Parker looked on. "Mother, please," Parker was saying. "You're making a scene."

"And why shouldn't I?" Mrs. Hill spluttered. "It's

been one thing after another since this whole thing began. Do you have any idea the kind of bad luck that comes from receiving a knife for a wedding gift?"

Mr. Hill tried to interrupt her tirade. "Now, Bonnie—" he said.

"It represents a broken relationship," Mrs. Hill went on, steamrolling her husband into silence. "A love that is destined to end." She punctuated this with a finger whipped across her neck in a slicing motion.

Parker winced. "It's just someone's idea of a stupid joke," he said. "It doesn't mean anything."

But it was clear that all these pranks were getting to him, and to the other guests as well. People were shuffling awkwardly to their feet and gathering their things, murmuring apologies before heading toward the door. Stupid joke or not, a dark cloud had settled over this wedding, and it wasn't going away until the person responsible was stopped.

I worked my way through the crowd over to Parker, who was sitting at the bridal table, his head in his hands. I put my hand on his shoulder and he looked up at me, his eyes glistening. "You're the detective. Tell me, why is this happening?" he asked. "Charlotte and I love each other. Why would anyone want to stop us from being together?"

"I have a few ideas," I replied, thinking of Tucker and Alicia, "but I still have some investigating to do. For now, though, you can't allow this person to get to you. By the end of tomorrow, you and Charlotte will be married, and there's nothing they can do to keep that from happening."

I felt someone's presence behind me and turned to find Piper and Morgan standing there, their faces creased with worry. "I just wanted to see if Charlotte was okay," Piper said, her eyes darting around the room. "I didn't see her leave."

"She went back to the inn with Bess and George," I told her. "She's going to be fine, I promise."

"Oh, good," Piper said, looking relieved.

"We're going to head back there too," Morgan said. "Do you two need a ride, or are you going to stay here for a while longer?"

"I'm going to help the rest of the bridal party collect the centerpieces and other things from the tables first," Parker said. "How about you, Nancy?"

"Well, I was planning on staying behind and giving you a hand with all this," I replied.

"That's so nice of you," Parker said gratefully. "Well then, we'll just grab a ride with someone after we're done, okay?"

I nodded. Piper and Morgan said their good-byes and followed the rest of the crowd out of the restaurant. I glanced outside, where a crescent moon had risen over the river, and I could see the winking lights of sailboats bobbing along on their way back to shore. If only the evening inside this room were as peaceful as the scene outside its windows.

After an hour of cleanup, Parker and I hitched a silent ride back to the inn with Mr. and Mrs. Hill. We all trooped, exhausted, back into the main lobby. "Thank you for your help, Nancy," Mr. Hill said before I turned to go upstairs. "I know you're not really part of the wedding, so it was mighty kind of you to stay behind and lend a hand."

"Of course," I said. "Even a stranger would see how much Charlotte and Parker love each other. I'm happy to do whatever I can to make sure their big day is just as they always dreamed it would be."

At my words, I saw Mrs. Hill blush. She looked at Parker's tired face and reached out to grab his hand. "I'm sorry I got so hot under the collar back there, sweetheart," she said to him. "I know Charlotte's a grade-A gal, and no amount of bad luck will keep you two lovebirds apart. Okay?"

Parker looked at his mother and smiled. "Thanks, Ma," he said.

I smiled too, glad that I could help put the wedding back on track—even in this small way. But a niggling worry in the back of my mind warned me that the culprit wasn't done with their mischief just yet.

Parker and his parents retired to their rooms on the first floor. Just as I was ascending the staircase up to mine,

Bess and George emerged from the hallway above and spotted me. "Nancy!" Bess exclaimed, rushing down the stairs to where I stood. "I'm so glad you made it back. We were starting to worry."

I sighed. "It took a while to finish cleaning up. How's Charlotte?"

Bess's shoulders slumped. "Okay, I guess. We just got her settled down for the night."

"Not the best way to spend the final hours before your wedding day," George muttered.

"No, it isn't," I said, frustrated. "In all the chaos, I never got a chance to talk to Alicia or Tucker more. I hope I can get a chance to do that in the morning— before the culprit can do any more damage!"

A moment later I heard someone shout "No!" from below us. It sounded a lot like Parker.

"I think," George said, "we might be too late."

The three of us tore down the rest of the stairs back to the first floor and down the hallway toward Parker's door. Before I could hammer on the door with my fist, it flew open, revealing Parker standing there, his eyes wide with panic.

"They're gone!" he cried, panting heavily.

"What are?" I asked.

"The wedding rings!" he replied.

❧

CHAPTER SEVEN

Diamonds Aren't Forever

MY HEART SANK TO MY KNEES. THE FEAR that had been lurking at the back of my mind had come to fruition—the person behind all these incidents had finally done something really serious. Something that could bring this wedding to a screeching halt.

I locked eyes with Parker, trying to bring him into focus. "Show me where you were keeping them," I said, keeping my voice level.

Parker nodded wordlessly and led Bess, George, and me into his room. It looked much like the other rooms in the inn, albeit a bit grander—it had lofty ceilings and a large fireplace in the center of one wall. On the floor of the wardrobe, Parker pointed out a small metal box, its lid ajar. A combination lock lay next to the box, also open.

"That's the inn's version of a lockbox?" George asked skeptically.

I agreed. The box and its lock were a pitiful excuse for security. The lock was made by a common household brand that anyone with a paper clip and the Internet could break into.

Parker shrugged. "This inn isn't normally a hotbed of criminal activity," he said. "There's no reason for top security here. The windows are all locked tight, and the door was bolted shut when I got here. I have no idea how this person got in or out." He walked over to the four-poster bed and slumped onto it. "What am I going to do? Those rings were priceless heirlooms. They've been in my family for six generations—they're part of Charleston's history, for goodness' sake!" I thought back to the gossipy article Bess had shown me on the plane. The reporter had been covering all aspects of the wedding, and they had mentioned something about the history—and the six-figure value—of the wedding rings.

"How am I going to tell my parents?" Parker was saying. "How am I going to tell Charlotte?"

It suddenly became clear that my investigation needed to get serious—and fast. I needed to find out who was behind all this and get those rings back ASAP, or else there might not be a wedding tomorrow. "Stay here—and for now, keep this news under your hat. We don't want the guests and bridal party to panic any more than they already have. Try to get some rest. In the meantime, there's something I need to figure out, once and for all."

I left Parker with his thoughts and pulled Bess and George out of the room with me. "After you guys change, come to my room," I said. "I hope you're not too tired, because we have work to do."

"Whatever it takes to help Parker and Charlotte," Bess replied.

George nodded. "I just don't understand how people are getting in and out of locked rooms!" she said as we climbed the stairs. "First the 'ghost' haunting people in the night, and now this! How are they doing it?"

"That's exactly what I want to find out," I said. "And since our culprit was able to get into my locked room, we should be able to figure out how they did it from there."

Once we got upstairs and changed out of our fancy dinner clothes, we got down to business. First we checked the obvious things—any trick locks on the windows or doors that might allow someone entry without a key. Nothing. I checked for a hidden entrance in the clothes closet or the bathroom, but that was a dead end too.

After ten minutes of searching, George decided to take a break. "Ugh!" she exclaimed, letting her head fall back against the wooden paneled wall with a thump. "Another dead end!"

I froze in place. "George," I said slowly. "Do that again."

George looked at me curiously. "Do what again?"

"Thump your head against the wall."

She blinked. "You've got to be kidding."

"Nope, totally serious."

George shrugged and thumped her head against the wall. It was just as I'd thought.

"What is it, Nancy?" Bess asked.

I walked over to another part of the wall in the bedroom and rapped on it with my fist. "Don't you hear the difference?"

Bess and George stared at me blankly. I walked over to where George was standing and rapped on the wall behind her, and then immediately again on another panel a couple feet away.

Bess's eyes widened as she recognized the subtle difference in tone. "It's . . . hollow!"

I grinned. "Bingo. I think we've found our hidden entrance. Now, all we have to do is figure out how to open it."

I peered closely at the wooden paneling, tracing around its edges with my fingertips, searching for some kind of release button. Sure enough, I found a circular knot in the wood on the right-hand side that wasn't flush with the rest of the wall. I pushed against it with my thumb, and it sank into the wall with a muted click. I took a step back as the whole panel swung inward, revealing a dark passage within.

"The plot thickens . . . ," George muttered.

"Do you have a flashlight?" I asked.

George whipped her smartphone out of her pocket and tapped its screen twice. A blinding beam of light shot out of the back and illuminated the first few dusty feet of the secret passageway. A mouse caught in the beam skittered across the wooden floor and out of sight.

"Eek!" Bess shrieked.

"The answers are in there, I just know it," I said. "Are you guys coming?"

"Wouldn't miss it!" George answered.

Bess sighed and nodded in agreement. "Maybe that's the only mouse in there," she said hopefully.

I doubted it, but that was what made Bess so great. I could always count on my friends to follow me into adventure—even if it was infested with mice!

With George's glowing smartphone in hand, I took the lead, with Bess following and George bringing up the rear. We walked silently, trying to avoid having the bare wooden planks squeak beneath our feet. About fifteen feet ahead of us, I saw a tiny circle of light shining on the left wall of the passage. I crept up to the little hole in the wall and set my eye against it. It gave me a full view of a very familiar room—the bridal suite! Charlotte herself was curled up in bed, reading a book by her bedside lamp. Then I noticed a panel similar to the one in my room that I presumed opened into Charlotte's room. "This is definitely how our ghost got in and out of the rooms unnoticed!" I whispered to the girls.

George sighed. "Too bad. 'Ghostly haunting' is so much more fun than 'peeping Tom.'"

We continued down the dark hallway. The passage seemed to follow a circuitous path through the inn, providing entrance into quite a few of the guest rooms, including Piper and Morgan's room, Alicia's room, and others who had been victims of the inn's "ghost" the night before. At the end of the passage, a final peephole revealed a glimpse of Tucker Matthews sitting in an armchair with a drink in his hand. He was leaning back, a smartphone pressed to his ear.

"You should have seen the look on his face," Tucker was saying, the side of his mouth lifted in a smirk. "His fiancée pulls a knife out of this pretty little box, and his whole 'Good evening, I'm Parker Hill' poise goes right out the window. I swear he looked like someone just ran over his dog." He chuckled, listening to the person on the other end. "I know, right? Parker thinks he's an angel without wings, but it looks like not everybody in this town agrees." Another pause. "Who sent the knife? Well, I—"

At that very moment, a scream broke the silence. I whirled to see Bess, her hands clamped over her mouth, trembling all over, staring with horror at a little gray mouse clinging to the front of her shirt.

"What was that?" Tucker exclaimed, dropping the

phone to his side and glancing around his room. The three of us froze, afraid to move or even breathe. After what seemed like an eternity, Tucker relaxed back into his chair and resumed his conversation. "Huh? Oh, I just thought I heard a weird noise coming from the walls. This is such an old place, it was probably just a mouse or something."

Little did Tucker know how right he was!

Meanwhile, the mouse had made it up to Bess's shoulder, where it was eagerly sniffing at the beads of her necklace. "Get it off!" she whispered fiercely.

George looked back and forth between us, making a *who, me?* gesture. Bess and I both nodded vigorously. George rolled her eyes and reached out to lift the tiny mouse by its tail off Bess's shoulder and onto one of the wooden beams that lined the walls of the passage. "Happy trails," she whispered, as the mouse scampered away. She turned back to us. "Both of you are utterly hopeless," she muttered.

"Sorry!" Bess whispered.

"It's okay," I said, though I was sorely disappointed

that Tucker had changed the subject and wasn't saying any more about who had planted the knife at the rehearsal dinner. But even without that information, Tucker was quickly becoming my prime suspect. I said as much to Bess and George once we were out of earshot of his room.

"He seemed a little too happy about all of Parker and Charlotte's misfortunes over the past couple of days," George murmured with a nod. "And not only that, it sounds like he has a theory about who's behind it! And who better to know than if he did it all himself?"

"I don't know, though," Bess whispered. "There's something about the pranks that just doesn't seem like Tucker's style. Changing the flower color? A knife in a fancy, gift-wrapped box? It all feels so . . . subtle. And Tucker doesn't strike me as the subtle type."

I had to agree. "You're right, it doesn't quite fit— but he's our best guess right now, and you can't ignore what we just overheard. Maybe he did those types of pranks just to throw people off his scent. Let's check out the rest of this passage before we head back to my room."

What we found at the end of the hallway was a hole in the floor with a ladder leading down to the first floor. The three of us descended the ladder as quietly as we could and found another peephole leading to Parker's room. "There you have it," I said, wiping a cluster of cobwebs from my hair. "Anyone with access to this passage could have gotten into Parker's room and stolen the wedding rings."

"So that narrows it down to the people in the rooms who have entrances," Bess mused. "But that still includes everyone who we already suspected—so not a lot of help."

"Better than nothing," George said. "At least we know we're on the right track."

The passage on the first floor was much smaller than the one on the second, so there wasn't a lot to see. At the end of the hall, I inspected the panel where another entrance would normally have been—they usually appeared at regular intervals. But this panel didn't have a peephole. I knocked on it lightly and found it hollow. "Where do you think this one leads to?" I wondered aloud. I took a couple of steps forward to inspect the edge of the panel and tripped over something at my feet.

"You okay, Nancy?" Bess asked.

"Yeah," I murmured, regaining my footing, and shone the smartphone light down at the floor. What I saw was a crumpled-up grocery bag, and its contents had spilled out onto the floor when I stumbled over it. I caught a glimpse of blue fabric and quickly snatched it up. "Look!" I exclaimed.

"What is it?" George said.

"This is the uniform the so-called ghost was wearing when he snuck into my room!" I pulled the whole bundle out of the bag and saw that it was some kind of old military costume. "It looks Civil War–era," I mused.

"Sounds like someone's trying to impersonate a ghost," George said. "But why?"

"I don't know," I said. I turned the bag upside down

to make sure nothing else was inside, and a single scrap of paper fluttered out. I picked it up and scanned the writing. "But this might help us figure it out."

It was a tattered newspaper clipping, yellowed with age. There were pictures of cars that looked at least seventy-five years old, as well as an ad calling for women to try out a new girdle that would make their waists look thinner. But most of the page was taken up by an article with the headline SPOOKY HAUNTINGS AT THE GREY FOX INN! It read:

> *Out-of-towners are once again hollering about the haunted happenings at the local Grey Fox Inn. Guests at the inn speak of a "uniformed gentleman" who makes visits to their rooms, opening doors, moving objects, and appearing to startled citizens in the wee hours of the night. Contrary to expectations, patronage of the inn has reached an all-time high, according to the owner, with the entire establishment fully*

booked through the end of the year. It seems
like everyone in Charleston is looking to get
a peek at the Ghost of Grey Fox Inn!

I handed the article over to Bess and George and tapped my chin in thought. From the sound of it, back then the inn had been haunted by the same kind of "ghost" as we were dealing with right now! But what did this have to do with Charlotte's wedding? Was the culprit hoping to use this tidbit of history to make their pranks seem like genuine ghost sightings? Were they hoping that Mrs. Hill's superstitious nature would be upset by all the bad juju and she would call off the wedding? If so, the plan had almost worked. It was only after it had been made clear that the ceremony was still on that the wedding rings had been stolen. Obviously the culprit needed to go to greater lengths in order to shut the whole thing down—so that's what they did.

Tucker Matthews, being in the news business, would have had access to a lot of this information. But then again, so would Alicia. In fact, considering that she'd worked at the historical society, Alicia would have had even greater access to the history of the inn; certainly newspaper clippings like this one. I couldn't zero in on Tucker as my main suspect without ruling out Alicia, and that meant taking a trip over to the historical society itself. I had a feeling that someone there might be able to shed more light on Alicia's feelings toward Charlotte and Parker—if she was the one behind all this, we needed to figure that out fast.

The three of us climbed up the ladder and picked our way through the dark, back to my room. After shutting the hidden panel behind us, we all collapsed onto chairs, dusty and exhausted.

"Ugh, look at the carpet," Bess said. "It looks like we tracked in more of that ash—just like the ghost did when he came in here."

"I'll try and clean it up a little tomorrow before the maid comes in," I said with a yawn. "In the meantime, here's our plan." I quickly laid out my thoughts about Alicia, and we agreed to make a trip to the historical society first thing in the morning, before any of the wedding activities began. "We need to start crossing off names," I finished, "and I think this is the best chance we've got at figuring out who did all this and getting the rings back in time."

Bess and George nodded. As we all said our good nights, I tried to sound more confident than I felt. Tomorrow was the big day. Charlotte and Parker surely had their vows all planned out, and I hadn't forgotten mine. For better or for worse—it was my job to save this wedding!

CHAPTER EIGHT

❧

The Rest Is History

BEEP! BEEP! BEEP!

I felt like my head had only just hit the pillow when my alarm clock went off. Blearily, I groped around until my hand hit the snooze button, and the room was silent once again. I collapsed back into the covers and yawned.

No time for snoozing, Nancy Drew, a voice in my head warned. *It's Saturday, the day of the wedding, and you have a bad guy to catch!*

Rubbing the sleep from my eyes, I hopped out of bed, stretched, and quickly dressed in the early morning light. Five minutes later I slipped out of my room into the stillness of the inn. It was early enough that all the guests were still asleep in their beds—a perfect time for the girls and I to sneak out and do some last-minute investigating. Parker could only keep the missing rings secret for so long—we needed an answer before the wedding had to be canceled!

Bess and George were already waiting for me in the lobby, looking about as tired and bleary-eyed as I felt. "Ready to go?" I asked.

"Absolutely," Bess said. "I want to catch this person, once and for all!"

Fifteen minutes later I pulled the convertible up to the Charleston Historical Society. It was a majestic white building, boasting wide columns and elegant domed windows. "It almost looks like the White House!" George observed.

"Let's hope we find what we're looking for," I said.

Inside, we found a high-ceilinged lobby, crowned with a wrought-iron chandelier above us. A welcome desk in the center of the room stood unmanned, the computer still switched off for the night. As a matter of fact, the whole building was as quiet as the sleeping inn, and I immediately began to worry that we had come too early—what if there was no one here to help us?

"Um, hello?" I called out. "Is anyone here?"

No answer.

I looked back at Bess and George. George shrugged and said, "Well, we're here, and the door was unlocked. It couldn't hurt for us to take a look around, could it?"

I glanced at Bess. "What do you think?"

Bess's mouth twisted with discomfort, but after a moment, I saw her expression set with steely resolve. "I think we don't have time to waste. If the answer's here, let's go and find it."

There were three corridors leading away from the main lobby. We decided to split up—Bess taking the left-hand passage, George taking the right, and me going down the stairs behind the welcome desk to the corridor straight ahead. "Look for anything you can find about Alicia Coleman," I said. "An old staff file, something on the computer system—anything." I turned to go, but on a whim, added, "And while you're at it, see if you can find anything else about the Grey Fox Inn." Something about that old newspaper article we'd found in the secret passage left me wondering if there was more to it than I had first imagined. We agreed to meet back in the lobby in ten minutes to share our findings.

I made my way to the staircase, trying as best I could to silence my steps on the gray stone tiles. At the bottom of the short stairwell, I found two public bathrooms, one door marked STAFF ONLY, and another one labeled RECORDS ARCHIVE. Unfortunately, the staff room was locked up tight—but the records room wasn't. I turned the doorknob to find a room filled with row after row of tall metal shelves, each one piled with brown filing boxes. It was dimly lit from three high-up windows at the back wall, the morning light illuminating thousands of dust motes that were thrown into the air when I opened the door. If there was any place to find what I was looking for, it had to be here!

Not risking turning on the lights, I flicked on my phone's flashlight, slipped into the room, and squinted up at the boxes on the shelves, searching the labels for anything about old staff members. Everything was arranged into categories and then ordered alphabetically—the row I was in seemed to be dedicated to famous citizens of Charleston. The next row was all about historic places in the city, and as I passed the box labeled Ga-Gr, I paused and decided to follow up on my earlier hunch.

Pulling the box from the shelf, I flipped through it until I found what I was looking for: a whole folder about the Grey Fox Inn. I opened it up and quickly flipped through the various newspaper clippings, letters, and other miscellaneous papers, not really sure what I was looking for.

Suddenly the room was flooded with fluorescent light, dazzling me and surprising me so much that the contents of the folder spilled onto the floor.

"Hey! Is somebody in here?" a man's voice called out. Hidden as I was between two rows of shelving, I couldn't see who it was. My heart leaped into my throat.

"I heard you! Whoever you are, come out before I call the police!" the man said. I could hear his footsteps advancing into the room. But he was behind one of the other shelves and couldn't see me, either.

Maybe if I just creep out while he's searching for me, I thought desperately, *I can come back in a little while and act like I just got here.*

I tiptoed toward the door and was almost home free when I felt a large hand clamp down on my shoulder. Despite myself, I let out a yelp.

"Nancy Drew?" a voice asked.

Puzzled, I whirled around and found myself face-to-face with Reggie Banks—Parker's best man! "Reggie!" I exclaimed, filled with relief. "Oh, I'm so glad it's you."

Reggie smiled uncertainly. "Yes, well—I have to ship off a rare document to the state museum in Columbia before Monday. May I ask what you're doing here . . . in the records room . . . alone?"

I felt my cheeks grow hot. "Well, it's actually a long story. But I could really use your help."

An instant later Bess and George tore into the room, out of breath. "Nancy, are you all right—oh!" Bess stopped short the moment she saw Reggie standing there next to me. "Why, hello," she said to him.

"Hi," Reggie replied. He looked between the three of us, utterly confused. "I really am missing something, aren't I?"

For the next few minutes, the girls and I filled Reggie in on everything that had happened since we'd arrived. He was staggered to hear that as of last night, the wedding rings were missing. "I can't believe Parker didn't tell me," he murmured, looking hurt. "I'm not only his best man, I'm his best friend!"

"Don't take it personally, Reggie," Bess said. "This only happened late last night, and we told him to keep it to himself—he didn't want any of the guests to find out."

Reggie nodded, and then turned to me. "You said you're some kind of amateur detective. So, who do you think is behind all of this?"

"I've got a couple of hunches," I replied. "But we need

more evidence to figure out which one is right. That's actually why we're here. We couldn't find anyone around when we arrived, so we decided to just poke around a bit on our own to look for information." I bit my lip. "Sorry about that."

Reggie grinned. "Don't worry about it. If I were in your shoes, I would have done the same thing to help out a friend. I'm just happy it's me who caught you and not my boss! He would have dragged you guys into the police station for trespassing—pretty faces or no."

Bess's cheeks turned pink at that. George rolled her eyes.

"But I still don't understand what you were looking for here at the historical society," Reggie finished.

"We need to know more about Alicia Coleman and her relationship with Charlotte and Parker," I replied.

Reggie's eyes went wide. "Alicia?! She's one of your suspects?"

"I'm afraid so," I said. "She's got plenty of reasons to wish that it was her marrying Parker today instead of Charlotte—and envy seems to be a pretty strong motive, given the incidents so far."

"I guess that's true," Reggie said after a moment. "But I just can't imagine Alicia being capable of this kind of thing. She's as hardcore about her career as Charlotte is and has a lot of good things going on in her life now—it doesn't seem likely that she would risk losing all of that just to sabotage her friend's wedding. And I can say that with confidence; Alicia and I worked together for several years, so I know her as well as anyone. Sure, she liked Parker when she met him—I mean, what woman wouldn't?" Reggie paused and gave me a serious look. "But once she saw how happy Charlotte and Parker were together, she backed off right away. You have to believe me, Alicia never did more than flirt with Parker—she would never do anything to hurt him or Charlotte. And anyway . . ." Reggie stopped and cleared his throat, suddenly looking uncomfortable. "After the rehearsal dinner last night, Alicia and I went for a drive around town in my car. We didn't get back to the inn until after midnight.

If the rings were taken sometime between the end of the dinner and eleven o'clock, it couldn't have been her."

George's eyebrows went up. "So you and Alicia are . . ."

Reggie looked at his shoes with a shy smile. "I'm not sure what we are. But I've always had a lot of respect for her, and seeing her again for this wedding, well . . . let's just say it brought those feelings back to the surface."

Bess clasped her hands together dreamily. "Oh, how romantic!" she said.

I sighed. So Alicia was another dead end!

"Well, we don't want to take up any more of your time," I said. "I know you've got a lot to do before the wedding starts. Let me just clean up this mess I made." I walked back to where I had dropped the Grey Fox Inn file and knelt down to gather up the papers from the floor. Some of the historical documents talked about how several people had died at the inn back in the nineteenth century—deaths that had led to the locals' belief that the inn was haunted. Years later, ghost sightings at the inn led to a surge in popularity, as described in the newspaper article we'd found back in the secret passage.

As I continued to pick up the papers, one in particular caught my eye. It was a familiar name that attracted my attention: John William Ross. It was a form transferring the deed to the inn from the previous owner to John William, about ten years ago. Paper-clipped to that form were a dozen others, all pertaining to events that had occurred at the inn since John William took ownership. Apparently, because the inn was a historic building, the city kept detailed records of anything that happened to the property. Looking through the papers, it seemed like the inn had endured one stroke of bad luck after another in the past decade. Hurricane damage, massive flooding, electrical malfunctions— the list went on and on. From the look of it, the inn was in major financial trouble.

My eyes flicked back and forth from the articles about the heyday of Grey Fox Inn, with its daily ghost sightings and guest lists reaching into the following year, and then back to the current state of things—no ghosts, no money. Well, no ghosts until three days ago, when a host of influential and wealthy guests arrived . . .

Suddenly a whole bunch of things clicked into place in my mind—things I hadn't even considered until that moment. "Girls!" I said, dashing around the shelves back to where they were standing.

"What? Did you find something?" George asked.

"I'm not sure how this fits in with everything else," I said, breathless. "But we need to get back to the inn right away. Reggie, would you mind if I borrowed this file for a while?"

Reggie shook his head. "Of course not. Whatever you need, Nancy. But what is it that you have to do at the inn?"

I slipped the file into my purse and pulled out my car keys. "There's someone there that I need to talk to."

CHAPTER NINE

~

Something Borrowed, Something Blue

THE GIRLS AND I SPED BACK TO GREY FOX Inn, and I was out of the car almost before I'd pulled the key from the ignition. I ran into the lobby and straight up to the front desk. The maid, Annabelle, was sitting there, typing something into the computer. "Where is he?" I asked.

"That man, Mr. Salazar?" she asked, her eyes wide.

"You're looking for him, aren't you? I knew someone would come looking for him!"

I cocked my head, puzzled. "Who? No, no—John William. Where's John William?"

Annabelle's face fell. "Oh. He's out in the garden." Without further explanation, she turned back to her work.

Salazar? What was that all about? I wondered. I shrugged at the girls and led the way out the back door that led to the lush garden at the rear of the inn. I asked Bess and George to keep their distance; I didn't want John William to be spooked by the sight of all three of us coming out to talk to him. "I still don't understand why you need to talk to him," George said.

"It's just a hunch . . . but I need to see where it leads," I replied.

They nodded and agreed to stay close but out of sight.

I went on alone, stepping through the grass, which was still wet with morning dew. It was incredibly peaceful there—clusters of magnolia and sassafras trees surrounded wide beds of flowers and bushes in bloom, and the only sound was that of birdcalls from the treetops. I almost felt guilty for disturbing such a beautiful scene with the confrontation I was about to have.

I saw him crouching down in one of the flower beds, applying some kind of fertilizer to the soil. He was wearing army-green coveralls and rubber boots, which were dusted with the same stuff he was spilling onto the ground.

"Ash," I said, breaking the silence.

John William started, almost falling over into an azalea bush. He clambered to his feet and faced me. "Oh, goodness, Miss Drew. You nearly made me jump out of my skin! I didn't hear you come up. What's that you said?"

"Ash," I repeated, pointing to the bag at his feet. "It's a good fertilizer, isn't it?"

"Sure is," John William replied. "Cheap, too. It works a treat on my roses."

"It also has a habit of sticking to your shoes," I continued.

John William looked confused, as if he'd heard me wrong. "Pardon?"

"Ash leaves a lot of tracks behind, is what I mean," I hinted, moving closer to him. "Sometimes in places that you don't want people to know you've been."

A few moments passed in silence, and John William's face went from red with exertion to a ghostly white. Finally he cleared his throat, choosing his words carefully. "Miss Drew," he said, "I'm not certain what you're suggesting, but—"

"I'm suggesting that you put on a blue Civil War–era soldier's uniform and used the secret passageways in the inn to terrorize the guests into thinking that the inn was haunted. In an attempt, I believe, to drum up more business and save the inn from financial ruin. My friends and I found the passageways, and we saw where each one led through those little peepholes. We were able to identify every secret entrance, except for one on the first level. And I'm fairly sure that last one leads to your office."

John William's mortified expression told me he was guilty, guilty, guilty.

"Please," he croaked, pulling the gardening gloves off his hands and putting them together, as if they were begging too. "You have to understand. I—I didn't mean any harm. If I don't fill up all the vacancies for the rest of the year, I'll be forced to sell the inn. This place has been in my family for generations! When your friend mentioned the old ghost sightings a couple days ago, I remembered all those old newspapers in the basement, talking about how popular the inn was when people thought it was haunted. My cousin down the street has a bunch of old uniforms from his war reenactment days, so I got the idea to borrow one and haunt the place myself. I figured it was worth a try. How could I not try, especially with that anchorman and all his newspeople staying right under my roof? They ate up all that ghost stuff like it was candy. If I got a story in the news about the inn, people would want to stay here, and I'd be able to keep this place running. You have to understand, young lady!"

Despite myself, I couldn't help but feel sympathy for John William. He was clearly desperate to save the inn that he loved so dearly, and sometimes people do crazy things for love. That thought reminded me of another important piece of this mystery.

"Now that I know you were the ghost sneaking into everyone's rooms, I have to know—did you have anything to do with the theft of the wedding rings?"

John William's eyes bulged out of his head, and his mouth dropped open in shock. "The wedding rings were stolen?"

His surprise was so authentic, I couldn't believe that he had committed the crime. But I had to be sure. "Where were you last night, between ten and eleven p.m.?"

John William frowned in thought, and then said, "I was in the kitchen, helping Annabelle wash up for the night. You can ask her yourself—she'll tell you I was there."

I nodded. I was happy to have figured out one part of this mystery, but the real culprit—the person intent on ruining Charlotte's wedding—was still at large. "John William," I began, "the rings are just the latest incident that has happened over these past few days. Someone has been sabotaging this wedding, and whoever it is somehow found out about the inn's secret passages and used them to break into Parker's room and steal the rings. I need to know if any of the guests could have seen you use the passages for your nightly hauntings. It's extremely important."

John William wiped the sweat from his brow with the back of his shaking hand. The sun was now beating down with full force through the tree cover, even though it was still fairly early in the morning. "Only one thing comes to mind," he said after a few moments. "Sometime during the first night you all arrived, after I had visited half a dozen rooms, I was rushing back down the passageway and tripped over something. I fell—made quite a racket, you see—and when I got up again, I checked through the peephole and saw someone looking directly my way. Whoever it was had turned on a bedside lamp, probably woken by the noise. He started walking toward the wall where the entrance to the passageway was. I got out of there right quick. Maybe he put two and two together and figured out that wall was hollow."

I stepped in closer. "You said 'he.' Did you see this person's face? Do you remember what room it was?"

John William looked pained. "It was late, and it was dark. I can't recall which room it was, and the man's face was backlit from the lamp—I couldn't make out any details through the peephole. But I can tell you, just from the shape of him, it was a man. Medium build, probably on the younger side from the way he moved."

The description was a perfect fit for Tucker Matthews. With Reggie having a pretty airtight alibi for Alicia, Tucker was the natural choice. "Thank you, John William," I said. "That's very helpful."

John William nodded, but it appeared he had something else on his mind. "Miss Drew, I have to ask—are you planning on telling anyone about my, uh, indiscretions?"

I considered his request. "I understand why you did what you did. But sneaking into people's rooms without their knowledge isn't right. If you want to save your inn, you need to find a different way."

The inn owner stared at his feet, looking ashamed.

"Here's what I'm going to do. Parker is a good guy, and he cares a lot about this town. He wouldn't want to see this inn be sold to some outsider and risk it being turned into a strip mall. He's got connections who can help you"—John William's eyes lit up—"but only if you never try this ghost thing again. I'm also going to tell Parker what you did, and if he ever finds out that you've haunted your guests again, it will be on the next morning's news."

John William smiled. "That's mighty fair of you, miss. I promise I'll do as you ask."

I returned the smile and turned back to the house to find Bess and George. Time was running out, and we had another confrontation ahead of us!

CHAPTER TEN

~

The Nose Knows

BY THE TIME WE GOT BACK INSIDE THE INN, the main lobby was crowded with family members and the bridal party, many of them already dressed for the big day. The ceremony was set to begin promptly at four p.m., and it was already creeping toward midday! That meant we had less than five hours to find those wedding rings.

As we made our way through the crowd, Parker caught sight of me and intercepted us at the foot of the staircase. "So? Any news?" he murmured, scanning the room to make sure no one else could hear us. "I can only keep this secret for so long. My mother has already asked to see the rings one last time to make sure they're polished, and I had to come up with an excuse why I couldn't give them to her!"

"I think we're getting close," I said. "I can't be certain, but I've narrowed the suspect list down and am going to ask someone a few questions right now."

Parker narrowed his eyes. "Who?" he asked, his voice low.

I swallowed, unsure of how wise it would be to reveal my suspicions to the anxious groom. "Well, like I said, I'm not sure of anything yet," I warned. "But right now I'm concerned that Tucker Matthews has a fairly strong motive."

Parker straightened up like he'd been jolted by an electric shock. "Tucker?!" he spluttered. "Why that ungrateful, backstabbing—" He started to climb the stairs, making a beeline for Tucker's room.

"No, Parker—wait!" I exclaimed. Bess and George exchanged worried looks, and we all ran up after Parker. But by the time we caught up with him, he had already stormed into Tucker's room. Tucker was standing at the mirror in his tuxedo shirt, his hands still poised at his neck, grasping at a half-knotted bow tie.

"What—what's going on?" he stammered, his eyes flitting back and forth between Parker's red face and our three panicked ones.

"How could you?" Parker said. "I know you were mad about not getting the evening news position, but how could you do this to me?" He advanced on Tucker and grabbed the groomsman by the front of his shirt. "It's my wedding, man!"

Tucker shoved Parker away, panting, his brows knotted in confusion. "Hey! Get your hands off me! Listen, Parker—I know weddings can make a guy crazy, but this is ridiculous. I have no idea what you're talking about!"

I stepped in between the two of them. "Parker, I know you're upset, but please, let me handle this." Scowling, Parker nodded reluctantly, and I turned to our suspect. "Tucker, someone has been causing trouble for this wedding, and we need to find out who it is."

Tucker readjusted his shirt and regarded Parker warily before focusing his attention on me. "You mean that knife prank at the rehearsal dinner?" he asked, and before he could stifle it, he chuckled.

I saw Parker rise to his feet, ready to attack Tucker once again, but I put a hand on his shoulder and willed him to stay back.

"You think that's funny?" Bess asked. She looked ready to jump on Tucker herself. "That knife scared Charlotte half to death!"

Tucker cleared his throat and quickly wiped the smirk off his face. "No, of course not. It's just . . . Parker, man. You've got to see it from my perspective. Ever since I met you, you were the golden boy. Everything always goes your way. I guess . . . it was just kind of satisfying, just for a second, to see that I'm not the only one who gets dealt a bad hand."

"So you did do it!" Parker snarled. "You planted that knife and stole the wedding rings!"

Tucker snorted. "Wait—what? The wedding rings are missing? I had no idea. . . ." Suddenly the reality of this confrontation seemed to dawn on Tucker, and his face paled. "Hold on a second. I may have enjoyed seeing you struggle at the dinner, but no way would I ever steal the wedding rings just to mess you up, Parker. Seriously, you've got to believe me!"

Parker's jaw was knotted with tension, but I could tell his resolve was cracking. Tucker did seem genuine . . . but if he wasn't our man, who was?

I had a few more questions for Tucker, but before I could continue, I heard a small voice behind me. "The rings . . . are gone?" it said. I whirled around to see Charlotte standing in the open doorway, wearing a blue cotton dress, her makeup done and her hair styled in an elaborate updo and fastened to her head with pearl-encrusted combs. She looked beautiful, but her face was a mask of horror.

"Sweetheart!" Parker exclaimed, and dashed to her side. "What are you doing here? I thought you were still with the stylist!"

"I . . . she finished up early, and I came looking for you. I heard you shouting over here and came to see what was the matter. I heard you say that the rings were stolen. Is this true?"

Parker looked pained. He hesitated for a moment before speaking. "It's true. It happened last night. I didn't want to upset you any more than you already were, so Nancy, George, Bess, and I decided to keep it to ourselves—we were hoping to find them before you needed to know."

"But you haven't," Charlotte said. Unlike the other times when bad things had happened, Charlotte seemed eerily calm, as if she had had been preparing herself for something like this. "Well, that's it then. We'll have to call off the wedding."

"No!" Parker said. "It's not too late—we still have time. Right, Nancy?"

I was about to say something when a strange aroma struck my senses. It was a fresh, pleasant scent—a little citrusy, and more than a little familiar. Why hadn't I smelled it before now? What in the room had changed since I first walked into it?

I walked a few steps closer to Charlotte, and the

scent intensified. Something in my mind clicked. "Charlotte," I said. "Are you wearing perfume again?"

Charlotte looked perplexed at this turn in the conversation. "Um, yes. It's the same one I was wearing when we first met. Is it bothering you?"

"No, not at all," I continued. "What kind of perfume is it?"

"It was actually a gift from my sister," Charlotte answered. "It's her favorite fragrance—she wears it all the time. It's a combination of cucumber and grapefruit, I think. I always thought it smelled like cleaning spray, but what do I know about perfume—Nancy, what's wrong?"

"Nothing, nothing at all," I said, but my heart was hammering. All this time, and I had overlooked something that was staring me in the face. But Parker was right, it wasn't too late to fix this. I turned to Tucker. "I'm sorry about all of this," I said. "If you want to blame someone, blame me, not Parker."

Parker looked surprised, as did George and Bess. "But Nancy," George muttered, "he was our top suspect.

If Tucker didn't do it, do you have some idea of who did?"

"I do," I said. "And I'm about to go find out if I'm right."

I left George and Bess behind with the bride and groom—the conversation I was about to have needed to be done delicately, so it was better I go in there alone.

I knocked on the door down the hall from Tucker's room. There was the sound of movement inside, and a moment later the door opened wide.

"Why, Nancy," Piper said. "To what do I owe the pleasure?"

"I just wanted to ask you about something," I said, trying to sound casual. "Can I come in?"

Piper smiled, but there was something different about her face. The smile seemed strained, and her eyes were a little red and puffy, as if she'd been crying. "Of course!" she said.

I walked into the room after her, taking in my surroundings as I did. Piper always had a pristine look about her—her hair always perfectly styled, her clothes crisply pressed, her makeup immaculate. Given all that, the state of her room was a bit of a surprise. Clothes were strewn across the bed in messy heaps, and the dresser was covered with the contents of Piper's purse and piled-up plates and glasses from room service. And despite the fact that the wedding was set to start soon, Piper's maid of honor gown was still hanging up on the bathroom door.

Piper saw my eyes ranging over the chaos of the room and looked apologetic. "Sorry about the mess," she said, still trying to sound cheerful. "Things have been a little hectic around here with all the pre-wedding excitement!" She brushed a pile of crumpled papers into the garbage bin, which I noticed was already full of wadded-up tissues, smeared with mascara.

"Are you all right, Piper?" I asked. "Is there something on your mind you want to talk about?"

Piper looked at me with a mixture of surprise and suspicion. "Me? No, I'm fine, of course! Why wouldn't I be?"

I gestured at the garbage bin. "It looks to me like you've been doing a lot of crying."

Piper glanced at the garbage bin as if it had betrayed her somehow. "Oh," she stammered. "Well, it's just an emotional time, you know. My little sister is getting married. I still can't believe it's really happening."

"Well, the way things are going, it might not be happening after all," I said, my voice level.

Piper swallowed hard and looked at me with apprehension. "What do you mean?" she asked.

"The wedding rings were stolen last night," I said.

I watched Piper's expression as I gave her the news. Unlike Tucker, her initial reaction wasn't shock. It was fear.

"Oh, I—that's terrible!" she said. "What are they going to do?"

"Nothing," I replied simply. "Because you're going to give them back."

Now Piper looked shocked. "M-m-me?!" she stammered. "Nancy, how could you say such a thing? What makes you think I would steal the wedding rings?"

"A lot of things, actually," I said. "In fact, I'm kicking myself for not seeing it sooner. All this time I was looking for someone who wanted to stop this wedding—someone who felt that 'it should have been me,' just like the message on the knife said. Alicia and Tucker both had reasons for being envious of Charlotte and Parker, and they always say that it's the people closest to the victim who are the likeliest suspects." I paused and looked meaningfully at Piper. "I guess I wasn't looking close enough. Bess had told me you were always the sister in the spotlight—the fashion model, the popular, charming girl of every boy's dreams. Nothing like Charlotte. So I can imagine what it must have felt like to find out that your bookish, shy younger sister was getting married before you. And to a famous, handsome news anchor, no less! It stung, didn't it?"

Piper's lower lip began to tremble, and a moment later, she crumpled into a wicker chair. "You have no idea," she whimpered. "I tried to hide my feelings, tried to be happy for her when she told me about the engagement. But all I could think of was all those boyfriends who never saw past my looks to notice that there's an actual person behind the makeup and nice hair. All those years, when I was crowned prom queen in high school, when I'd daydream of my fairy-tale wedding—only to have my little sister, who never cared about anything except what she read in those dusty old books, to get it before me. You're darned right it stung! And Charlotte didn't even realize what she had. She was all worried about how it all might interfere with her studies. Can you believe that? I dreaded this wedding, but I couldn't allow anyone to know it. I only let my emotions out when no one was around, like when I was waiting in the Charleston airport for my ride to the inn. That's when I met Morgan."

I cocked my head, confused. "You only met Morgan a few days ago? But I thought you two had been dating for a while now."

Piper chuckled humorlessly. "Another lie. He sat next to me while I was waiting, and we started to chat. I told him how I was going to my sister's wedding alone, and he offered to be my date."

I raised my eyebrows. "Just like that?"

Piper shrugged. "He was handsome. It was romantic. You know how it is."

I blinked. I didn't really know how it was.

"Anyway, I told him the whole sob story, and he kind of gave me the idea to do these pranks—just a little revenge to get back at my sister. It was exciting—I had fun wrapping that gift for her, let me tell you!"

"A little too much fun," I said. "Getting your perfume all over the box is what gave you away. I smelled it when we met Charlotte on that first day; she had it on even though she told us she normally doesn't wear perfume. I didn't put two and two together right away when I smelled it again on the gift box, but the third time's a charm. Charlotte had it on again just now, and when I asked her about it, she told me you'd given it to her. Your favorite fragrance."

Piper shifted uncomfortably in her seat. "Guilty as charged. I usually give the gift-wrapping a little spritz as a final touch—I guess I should have skipped that step this time. Some habits are hard to break."

She sighed. "Like I said, I got so into the fun of the pranking, I forgot that I was really hurting people. But once I saw the look of horror on Charlotte's face when she opened the box at the dinner, I—I lost my taste for revenge."

I crossed my arms. "I'm sorry you haven't found the romance you've been searching for. But that's not Charlotte's fault. You had no right to take out your anger on her during such an important event in her life."

She looked up at me, a desperate look on her face. "I know. I know . . . I've been awful. You have to believe me, Nancy! I love my sister. I don't know what came over me, but I'm done with it now. I just hope it's not too late to make things right."

"It isn't too late," I said. "Just give me back the wedding rings, and Charlotte's big day will be saved!"

"I would!" Piper replied. "But there's just one problem. . . ."

"What's that?" I asked.

"I don't have them."

My heart plummeted. "Then who does?" I asked. Suddenly, I heard the door open behind me.

"Well, well, well," came a low voice behind me. "Just the two ladies I wanted to see."

I whirled around to see Morgan standing in the doorway.

CHAPTER ELEVEN

~

The Bachelor Did It!

MORGAN. THE MOMENT I LAID EYES ON HIS smug, cunning face, certain pieces of this puzzle began to fall into place.

Piper rushed up to him, wringing her elegant, manicured hands. "Listen to me," she said, desperation in her voice. "Nancy knows. About everything. Please, I keep telling you, I don't want to do this anymore! I let my jealousy get the best of me. Just give the rings back, and the wedding can go on—we can pretend none of this ever happened. It's not too late!"

Morgan looked at Piper like he felt sorry for her. "Oh, you poor little thing," he said. "Of course it's too late." And with that, he turned around and shut the door behind him. I heard the sharp click of the dead bolt, and suddenly my pulse quickened.

"Open the door," I said, trying to keep my voice even.

Morgan chuckled. "Mrs. Hill was right about you, Nancy," he said, facing me. "You were bad luck from the start. Sticking your nose where it doesn't belong, messing with other people's business. I was fully prepared to handle this one"—he gestured at Piper—"if she became unmanageable, but now I have to deal with both of you." He tsked and shook his head. "This con has turned out to be more trouble than it was worth."

Aha. Another piece of the puzzle fit into place.

"Con?" Piper exclaimed, confused. "What do you mean, con? I thought you were doing all this for me!"

"I hate to say this," I said to Piper. "But I don't

think this was ever about you." I turned to Morgan. "Isn't that right, Mr. Salazar?"

Morgan raised his eyebrows. "Impressive," he said. "Where did you hear that name? It's not my real one, by the way."

"Annabelle, the maid, seemed to recognize you when she saw you that first day. At first I thought it was nothing, but then when I was looking for John William, Annabelle mistakenly thought I was after someone named Mr. Salazar. Someone she expected people to come looking for—as if she knew from personal experience that he was trouble. As there's no one else in the bridal party or immediate family with that name, it had to be you. Which tells me that you must have some kind of reputation around here. A con man. My guess is: you were at the airport looking for an easy target, and you found Piper. Rich, beautiful, troubled . . . and offering you a free ticket into Charleston's wedding of the year. Perfect."

"What can I say?" Morgan replied. "Guilty as charged."

Piper looked mortified. "So . . . so . . . you, and me, and everything—it was all a lie?"

The conman shrugged. "Sorry, honey," he said. "Love hurts, I guess. Anyway, you got to see your nerdy sister and that pretty-boy TV anchor cringe. That's what you wanted, isn't it? You couldn't have pulled off any of those stunts without me. So my side of the deal was these little sparklers." Morgan pulled a box out of his pocket and opened it to reveal two rings nestled inside. The bride's was a delicate circlet, encrusted with at least a dozen tiny diamonds that twinkled in the sunshine; the groom's was a thick gold band, covered with whispery engravings of whorls and curlicues. By the look of them, they were definitely worth a small fortune.

Morgan saw me staring at them and grinned. "Not bad, eh? Once I found out that Piper was the sister of the girl marrying into the Hill family, I knew I had to get myself invited to this wedding. Everyone in Charleston knows that these rings are worth a pretty penny, thanks to all the news coverage this event received. I just had to bide my time until I got the chance to get my hands on them."

That brought me to another part of this mystery. "The man who caught John William using the secret passages—that wasn't Tucker Matthews, was it? It was you."

"Right again!" Morgan said with a nod. "I hadn't really figured out my angle that first night, but when I saw that creep sneaking around in a costume and scaring people—well, it was the perfect opportunity for me. Everyone was so excited about haunted this and haunted that, they hardly even noticed when little things started to go missing. They just thought it was the ghost. And once I saw that Parker was still at Indigo Blue after the rehearsal, I knew it was the perfect time to snatch the rings."

Piper lowered herself into a chair, her face drained of hope. "Poor Charlotte," she murmured, as if the reality of everything that had happened had finally sunk in. "What have I done?" She put her head in her hands and began to cry.

A look of concern crossed Morgan's face, and he walked over to the minibar and poured some water into a glass. He handed it to Piper, who looked up at him with mascara-stained cheeks and grasped it gratefully. "I wish it didn't have to be this way, honey," he said. "But I can't change what I am." Piper sucked in a shuddering breath and drank the entire glass of water in one gulp.

I glanced back at the door. It was a good eight feet away from where I was standing, but Morgan was focused on Piper for the moment and had his back to me. If there was any chance for me to get out of here, it was now.

I darted toward the door and scrambled to unlock the dead bolt, but just before I could grasp the doorknob, I felt two strong arms wrap around my waist and wrench me away from the door. Morgan whipped around and tossed me roughly to the floor. Luckily, the room was carpeted, so the landing just stung my arms and back but didn't knock me out cold.

"Not so fast, Nancy," Morgan growled, standing over me. "I can't have you telling all my secrets, now can I?"

I got to my feet as quickly as I could, trying to

reassess my situation. I looked over at Piper and gasped. She was slumped over in the chair, her head lolling limply to the side, her eyes half-closed. "What did you do to her?" I demanded.

"Oh, don't worry," Morgan replied, pushing a lock of silky hair back into place. "I just put a little something in her drink to make her sleep for a while. You can't very well expect me to wrangle both of you at the same time—that would be extremely troublesome. Now, enough of these games; it's time to go."

Before I could think of another way out, Morgan had lunged at me, grabbing one of my arms and twisting it behind my back. I struggled, driving the heel of my foot hard into his knee, but not before he had slipped a pair of plastic zip-tie handcuffs around my wrists and tied a handkerchief around my mouth, muffling my screams. He stumbled back in pain, but still managed to keep a hold on my arm. "Nice try," he said through gritted teeth. "But you're not getting away that easily. I need time to get these rings to a buyer, collect my money, and disappear before you're going anywhere."

Where does he think he's taking us, anyway? I wondered. *We're in a locked room. He can't possibly think he can get out of here without getting caught.* But even as I thought it, my stomach turned over. I knew exactly what Morgan had in mind, and it wasn't good.

Sure enough, Morgan walked over to the back wall of the room and removed a hanging tapestry from its place. He depressed an almost invisible button in the wall behind it, and a panel opened up to reveal the secret passage within, just as it had in my own room. "That panel into the owner's office leads right to a back door to the parking lot," Morgan said. "I'll just pop you in the trunk and come back for the little lady there"— he tilted his chin toward Piper—"and we'll be good to go. It's not a pretty plan, but it will have to do." With a grand gesture, Morgan swept his arm toward the dark hallway and said, "After you."

Morgan got behind me and nudged me forward into the passage. My mind was racing, desperately considering every avenue of escape, eliminating them as I went along. The closer I got to that car, the fewer options I had. Whatever I was going to do, I needed to do it before Morgan got me into that trunk.

I walked slowly, pausing after every step, but Morgan kept pushing me forward, not allowing me to stall enough to think. The dark passageway was silent—most of the guests must already be downstairs in the main room, blithely drinking their iced teas and chatting while a kidnapping was occurring right above their heads!

How many peepholes had we passed so far? Three? Four? I remembered that the bridal suite had been three panels away from my room, and Piper's room was right across from mine. If we were looping around, we should be passing the bridal suite at any moment now. If luck was on my side, George and Bess might still be with Charlotte in her room. If only I could let them know I was here . . . give them a sign! But with my hands tied, my mouth gagged, and Morgan watching my every move, that was going to be difficult.

Suddenly a lightbulb went off in my head.

I couldn't scream, but Morgan still could.

As soon as we were passing the panel that I thought might lead into the bridal suite, I pretended to sway on my feet and groan, as if I were feeling faint.

"Hey," whispered Morgan. "What's wrong with you? Keep walking!"

But I only groaned again in response, and, steeling myself for the pain that was surely going to follow, let my body go completely limp and toppled to the ground.

I landed on my back, pinching my arms under me in a way that made tears leap into my eyes. But I bit back against the pain and stayed completely still, as if I were unconscious.

Morgan froze at the sound of my body falling, and for a few moments he waited, listening for any sounds from the rooms around us. But when nothing happened, he relaxed again.

As for me, I started to worry. If there were people in the bridal suite, shouldn't we be hearing their voices by now? Would my plan all be for nothing? There was only one way to find out . . .

Muttering quietly under his breath, Morgan began to reach down for me, ready to hoist me up onto his shoulders. But at the last moment, when he was most vulnerable, I reared up and kicked him, as hard as I possibly could, right between the legs.

And just as I'd hoped he would, Morgan howled.

It was probably only seconds, but it felt like an eternity later, when the wall opened and the dark passageway was flooded with blinding light. And in the middle of the light, I saw the silhouette of a man standing there—Parker.

"What the—" he stammered, trying to comprehend the scene before him. Morgan was doubled over in pain, and I was lying on the floor next to him, bound and squinting into the light.

"Nancy! He's got Nancy!" George was saying. She was standing next to Parker, one hand on the wall—she must have been the one to open the panel when they heard Morgan scream.

Parker's expression instantly changed from confusion to fury, and he grabbed Morgan by the collar and yanked him out of the passageway and into the bridal suite. Bess, who had been standing with Charlotte in the open door to the bridal suite, came running over to me and pulled the gag from my mouth. "Are you okay, Nance? What happened?"

Still wincing from the pain of my fall, I got out the only words that really mattered. "Check . . . his . . . pocket!"

Parker dug his hand into Morgan's jacket pocket and pulled out the little square box. Inside, the two wedding rings sat unharmed in their plush satin cushion, sparkling in the sun. Charlotte gasped. George grinned. Parker clicked the box shut with one hand and turned his attention back to Morgan, whose face was white with agony. "I can explain . . . ," he sputtered uselessly.

"Consider yourself uninvited," Parker said, and socked Morgan right in the jaw. The con man dropped like a stone. Parker rubbed his knuckles and turned to Charlotte. "Darling, if you wouldn't mind, call the police. And tell them to make it quick—we don't want to be late to our own wedding."

Charlotte smiled, her face sparkling even brighter than the diamonds in that little box, and pulled a smartphone from her purse on the vanity. And at that moment, with that smile, I knew it was finally over.

An hour later, after the police had quietly escorted Morgan out of the inn, Bess, George, and I were sitting together in the bridal suite, watching Charlotte adjust her wedding veil in the vanity mirror.

"I can't believe this is finally happening," Charlotte said to her reflection. "It feels too good to be true."

Bess smiled. "Parker sure knows how to handle a crowd. He did an amazing job distracting the guests downstairs while the police took Morgan away. I don't think a single person realized anything was amiss!"

"That was pretty amazing," Charlotte agreed, "but none of this would have been possible if it weren't for you, Nancy." She turned to me. "I don't know how to thank you for what you did."

I blushed. "I'm just glad you all went into the bridal suite when you did. You guys saved me."

George elbowed me playfully. "Oh, don't start changing the subject now, Miss Humility. It's all in a day's work for our resident supersleuth. Do you want another ice pack, Nance?"

I was about to decline, but instead I handed the melted bag of ice back to George and nodded. "That would be great, thanks." My wrists were still smarting from that fall. Just as George was crossing the room to the mini-fridge for more ice, there was a knock on the door. Bess got up to answer it. Standing in the doorway, looking haggard and ashamed, was Piper.

I had already filled Charlotte and the other girls in on what had transpired in Piper's room—how she'd met Morgan in the airport, how he'd convinced her to play those pranks, how she knew about the theft of the wedding rings but had wanted to confess before everything with Morgan went sour. But after the police arrived, Charlotte hadn't had a chance to talk to Piper before the officers had led her outside for questioning.

The girls and I looked back and forth between

the two sisters, unsure of what was going to happen next.

Piper took a hesitant step into the room, unable to meet her sister's gaze. "I . . . um, the police let me go. They said that Morgan would be going to jail for a long time. Apparently he's done this kind of thing to other people before. He's . . . wanted for theft, fraud, some other stuff."

Charlotte said nothing. The tension in the room was almost unbearable.

Piper took a steadying breath and went on. "But that's not the point, is it? The point is, I let him convince me to do those things. Convince me to hurt you, Char. And I don't know if you'll ever be able to forgive me for that. I don't know if I deserve to be forgiven. I let my jealousy blind me, and look what happened!" Piper's voice began to falter, but she steadied herself and went on. "Anyway, there's nothing I can say except: I'm so, so sorry. And if you never want to see me again, I'd understand."

Piper sighed and turned away, about to walk out

of the room. But before she could, Charlotte picked up her dress and dashed forward to stop her. "Piper, wait," she said, grabbing her sister by the shoulder. "What you did was—" She hesitated. "Mean. And dangerous. And incredibly stupid." Piper looked like she wanted to disappear into the floor. "But . . . you're still my sister. And it's my wedding day. And despite everything, I need you."

Piper looked up, a spark of hope in her eyes.

"Will you stand beside me, Piper?" Charlotte asked.

Piper's face crumpled. "Oh, Charlotte!" She wrapped her sister in an embrace, and the two of them cried and hugged and cried until it was time to go to the church.

Bess dabbed at her eyes with a handkerchief. "It's just so beautiful," she said, sniffling.

George watched the whole scene with a mixture of confusion and amazement. "Weddings!" she muttered, shaking her head. "I'll never understand them."

CHAPTER TWELVE

❦

Let Them Eat Cake

"DO YOU, CHARLOTTE GOODWIN, TAKE Parker Hill to be your lawfully wedded husband? To have and to hold, in good times and bad, in sickness and in health, for as long as you both shall live?" The reverend paused, looking expectantly at Charlotte. His white robes seemed to glow in the rays of the late-afternoon sun, which poured through the stained-glass windows of the church, coloring everything and everyone at the wedding ceremony in a warm, almost magical light.

I sat three rows back from the front pew with

George, who was taking photos with her phone and sniffling. When I stole a look at her, she quickly wiped at her eyes and snapped, "What? It's allergies."

I chuckled to myself and turned back to the ceremony. Bess was standing at the front with the other bridesmaids, looking perfectly lovely in a peach-colored gown and clutching a bouquet of white roses. Luckily, Charlotte had been able to correct the flower order just in time. All around me, every seat in the entire church was filled, but the whole place was silent as we all waited for Charlotte's answer.

Charlotte glanced back at Piper, who was standing just beside her. Piper reached out and grasped her sister's hand, just for a second, before letting go. Her eyes glistening, Charlotte turned back to face Parker, who looked dashing in his navy-blue tuxedo, and said, "I do."

A moment later I heard a sob burst forth from someone in the front row. I craned my neck to see Mrs. Hill and Mrs. Goodwin clutching each other and weeping, fistfuls of tissues in their hands. I smiled. It looked like even those two families could put their differences behind them when true love was at stake.

The reverend waited for the weeping to subside, then continued, "And do you, Parker Hill, take Charlotte Goodwin for your lawfully wedded wife? To have and to hold, in good times and bad, in sickness and in health, for as long as you both shall live?"

Parker grinned his winning TV grin, and from the corner of the church, cameras flashed and clicked to capture the moment. Parker's entire crew from the news station was there—photographers, cameramen, and reporters—covering the wedding. Tucker Matthews had been desperate to tell the station about all that had happened with Morgan: the stolen rings, the attempted kidnapping, the heroic rescue, but Parker had refused to let it go public. "I don't want my wedding to be remembered as a flashy sound bite," he had said to Tucker. "It isn't about that. It's about me and Charlotte."

Tucker was disappointed, but he understood. After everything had been cleared up, the two young men had made amends, promising to share a couple of drinks at the reception. Plus, Parker and Tucker agreed to work together on a special feature about the Grey Fox Inn, highlighting its history and importance to the city—which would certainly help John William's bottom line.

Parker waited until the cameras had stopped flashing, and took a moment to gaze at the face of his bride-to-be. "More than anything in the world, I do," he finally said.

The reverend placed their hands together and, his voice echoing through the church, announced, "Then by the power vested in me by the great state of South Carolina, I now pronounce you man and wife. You may kiss the bride!"

With that kiss, the whole of the church rose to their feet, applauding the happy couple. As Bess proceeded back with the other bridesmaids and groomsmen, she grabbed our hands and pulled George and me along with her. "C'mon, you two!" she said over the din of music and cheers. "It's time to party!"

* * *

Two hours later, in a waterfront ballroom nearby, I was sitting at the wedding reception, watching a crowd of party guests do the electric slide. "Nancy!" Bess shouted over the din. "Come and dance!"

I laughed and waved her away. Line dancing was never really my thing—I always ended up bumping into people or stepping on their toes. Just ask Ned.

I thought I had escaped the pull of the dance floor when I felt someone grab my hand. It was Tucker Matthews! "This party ride needs you on it, Nancy Drew!" he said in my ear.

I shook my head. "Maybe later!"

Tucker regarded me with a mischievous grin. "Earlier today you accused me of being a thief and got me roughed up by a lead anchorman—I think you owe me one!"

Well, he has a point there, I thought, and allowed Tucker to drag me into the throng of dancers and join in. We snuck in next to Reggie and Alicia, who had been joined at the hip since the ceremony ended. From the look of them, it seemed like this wedding might mark the beginning of another beautiful relationship!

After twenty minutes of nonstop dancing—during which I managed to avoid crushing any toes—the DJ came over the sound system and announced that it was time to cut the cakes. After the bride and groom sliced into the amazing three-tiered, fondant-sculpted, edible masterpiece that Carla from Sugar & Spice Bakery had concocted, Charlotte called all her bridesmaids over to the next table for the cutting of the charm cake. George and I walked over with Bess to get a better look; from what Carla had said about the tradition, it sounded like a lot of fun.

As the bridesmaids all gathered around the table behind the cake, I felt a hand on my arm. It was Piper. "Nancy, I want to thank you again for everything you did to help Charlotte"—she paused—"and to help me. I don't know what would have happened if you hadn't figured everything out in time. Morgan would have put me in that car, and I could have ended up . . . well, who knows where?" She looked down at her shoes and sighed. "Anyway, I made a really big mistake letting him get inside my head, and because of you, I had the opportunity to make it right, and to be here today with my sister."

I squeezed Piper's shoulder. "I'm glad everything worked out the way it did," I said.

"Anyway," Piper continued, "I want you to go and pull my ribbon for the charm cake. It's the least I can do. You deserve to be a special part of this wedding—it wouldn't have happened without you!"

Delighted, I let myself be led to the table with the other bridesmaids. Charlotte gave me a hug as I approached. "Piper told me that she wanted you to take her place. Go ahead, Nancy—you pull the first ribbon!"

I looked at the cake. Like the wedding cake, it was covered in white fondant, with a nest of beautifully sculpted peach-colored roses and green leaves crowning it. Sprouting out of the layers of the cake were four silk ribbons, one for each bridesmaid and one for the maid of honor. With every eye on me, and cameras flashing, I reached out, picked one of the ribbons, and pulled. Out of the thick icing emerged a small silver pendant, about the size of a quarter.

"What is it? What is it?" Bess squealed from behind me, craning her neck to look.

I picked up a napkin and wiped away the icing. The pendant was a tiny ship's anchor. "What does it mean?" I asked, turning to Charlotte.

Charlotte smiled. "The anchor represents adventure," she said.

From across the table, George laughed. "Well, of course it does!" she exclaimed. "When you're with Nancy Drew, there's always bound to be an adventure!"

Dear Diary,

WOW—TALK ABOUT THE WEDDING OF the year! For all the trouble it took to get there, the wedding went off without a hitch. Everyone had a wonderful time, and the girls and I even got to be on TV! Of course, it was just a shot of us dancing to "We Are Family" with Parker and Charlotte, but it was still quite a thrill for us and our families back home.

Bess, George, and I are sunning ourselves on the beach, enjoying our last day here before we fly back home to River Heights in the morning. George wanted to do the Charleston Ghost Walk tonight, but I told her I'm going to pass. I think I've had quite enough of ghosts for a while!

READ WHAT HAPPENS IN THE NEXT MYSTERY

IN THE NANCY DREW DIARIES,

Riverboat Roulette

"George, you've counted that money eight times," my friend Bess Marvin said from the passenger seat of my car. "I promise, you have enough for the entry fee."

"I just want to make sure," her cousin George Fayne said from the backseat, where she was rifling through a large stack of twenty-dollar bills. I slowly rolled up my driver's-side window as I inched forward in rush-hour traffic. The last thing we needed was for any of George's hard-earned money to fly out the window.

Bess gave me an exasperated look. I shrugged and gave a half smile. Bess knows that George gets fixated on things she's passionate about, and there are few things George is more passionate about than poker.

Her dad taught her when she was five and now she plays every weekend with her family; she even watches the *World Series of Poker* on TV.

Bess is very even-keeled and doesn't tend to become obsessed with things like games or new gadgets the way George does. In a lot of ways George and Bess are polar opposites, even though they're incredibly close. George would wear jeans and a T-shirt every day if she could, while Bess is a bit of a fashionista. (Take tonight, for example: Bess had spent weeks looking for the perfect dress for the charity event we were attending before picking a gorgeous asymmetrical ruby-red gown, while George wore the same black pantsuit she wore to any event that required dressing up.) George loves technology, while Bess would rather send a paper letter than an e-mail. In general, I fall between them— for instance, I didn't buy a new dress for tonight, but I did spend a good hour going through my closet choosing which dress to wear.

When it comes to obsessive behavior, however, I'm probably closer to George. I'm an amateur detective;

I solve mysteries around town, like if something goes missing or someone is being blackmailed. When I'm on a case, I can barely think about anything else.

"Okay," George announced. "It's confirmed that I have the entry fee." She carefully put the money back in her wallet.

"I can't believe how much money you were able to save," I told George. "I don't think I've ever seen that much cash in one place before."

"Well, if everything goes according to plan," Bess said, "you should see a lot more tonight. My mom told me that this event is supposed to bring in over a hundred thousand dollars."

We were headed to the annual charity casino night hosted by River Heights's Pet Crusaders, the animal rescue organization for which Bess's mom—and George's aunt—sat on the board. We went every year and it was always fun—getting dressed up, eating fancy food, and watching the big poker tournament. However, this was the first year we were allowed to actually *enter* the tournament, rather than just watch it. Bess and I weren't big poker players, but we were excited to support George.

"That's a lot of money for Pet Crusaders!" I said to Bess. "I hope your mom is happy."

"Yeah," Bess replied with a smile. "It's more than they've ever raised before."

"Probably because it's the first time they've gotten Brett Garner to attend," George suggested.

I saw that Bess was trying hard not to smile. "I'm not sure Brett's as big of a draw as you think he is, George."

George looked at us wide-eyed. "But Brett Garner is one of the most famous poker players in the United States. He's won the *World Series of Poker* twice!"

"I know he's impressive," I said. "I'm just not sure the average River Heights citizen knows who he is. Professional poker is still a pretty niche game."

"If Ned were here, he'd back me up," George grumbled. Ned Nickerson, my boyfriend, shared George's love of poker. Unfortunately, he was out of town at his cousin's wedding.

"I think the event is so popular because it's on a boat this year," I said. For the first time, the gala was being held on the *Delta Queen*, a refurbished riverboat that was originally built in the late 1800s. Back then it had transported people up and down the river in luxury. It used to have a full restaurant; entertainment, including a casino floor; and dancing with live music. Now it just hosted short dinner cruises. It was well known in River Heights that Buddy Gibson, the owner and captain, had saved up for years to buy and restore the *Delta Queen*. His stepdad had been a riverboat captain and Buddy had always dreamed of continuing the family tradition. It took him close to two years to get it back into working condition; there was a big story in the *River Heights Bugle* when it had finally opened. Tickets were notoriously hard to secure.

Bess grinned. "Mom was really proud when she was able to rent it. Apparently Buddy gave her a great rate." Bess leaned in to whisper, even though it was just the three of us in the car. "Seriously, my mom got him to let Pet Crusaders use it for almost nothing."

I smiled, then glanced over and noticed Bess clenching her fist, something I knew she did only when she was stressed out. If we were using George's poker language, it would be her "tell," or signal that something was wrong.

"Are you nervous, Bess?" I asked

"A little," Bess replied. "It's just that my mom has been working so hard on this event that I want it to go perfectly. Margot, the head of Pet Crusaders, is really high-strung. She's been flying off the handle if anything is even slightly off. The other night I saw my mom crying; Margot yelled at her because the caterers were going to switch green olives for black olives on one of the appetizers."

"I've seen Margot at the galas but she's always rushing around, so I've never actually met her. But now I have to meet her to tell her not to mess with my aunt," George muttered.

Bess looked up at her in alarm. "Don't say that! Margot's going about it the wrong way, but I understand why she's putting so much pressure on this event.

She's going to use the money to open a second no-kill shelter in River Heights. That's twice the number of dogs and cats that will be saved every year."

George looked chagrined. "Great! Now I sound like a heartless monster."

We pulled into the parking lot, hopped out of the car, and made our way to the boarding area. Well-dressed couples ambled about, heading toward the bright, white boat. The light from the setting sun reflected off the vessel's surface. Three stories high, each deck looked almost like an elongated tier of a wedding cake. My favorite detail was the carved railings around each deck that, from a distance, looked like lace. At the front, large steam pipes stood tall, and a red paddle wheel was at the boat's rear. It looked both delicate and strong.

Bess led us through the maze of cars, scanning the parking lot for her mother.

"It looks like a good turnout," I noted.

All of a sudden, a voice called out, "Bess! Over here!"

We turned to see Bess's mom waving at us and hurried over to her.

"I'm so glad you girls could make it," Mrs. Marvin said.

"We wouldn't miss it," I said.

"There's no way I would skip out on seeing Brett Garner," George said enthusiastically.

"Or any event that supports the lives of animals," I added.

"We got our cat, Joey, from Pet Crusaders, and he's the best," George agreed.

"So how's it going so far, Mom?" Bess asked.

"Oh, well, you know Margot. There was a lot of drama getting everything ready this afternoon, but once we shove off I'm sure it will be fine."

Mrs. Marvin led us up the metal boarding ramp. I was about to hand my ticket to the usher when a tall woman with short red hair came marching toward me. Her hair was pushed back so it looked like flames coming off her head. As she tore down the ramp, her black shawl billowing behind her, she reminded me of a picture of an evil faerie I'd seen in a book of Irish mythology. I found myself taking a step back, my hands reaching instinctively for my friends.

"You," she said with a hiss, "are not allowed on this boat."